MARGARET MOUNSDON

ISLAND
MAGIC

Complete and Unabridged

LINFORD
Leicester

First published in Great Britain in 2017

First Linford Edition
published 2018

A catalogue record for this book is available
from the British Library.

ISBN 978–1–4448–3717–9

Published by
F. A. Thorpe (Publishing)
Anstey, Leicestershire

Set by Words & Graphics Ltd.
Anstey, Leicestershire
Printed and bound in Great Britain by
T. J. International Ltd., Padstow, Cornwall

This book is printed on acid-free paper

1

'You must have heard of Giovanni Petucci. He's huge.'

Vanessa Blake smiled at her sister's incredulity as she confessed her ignorance.

'Sorry.'

'Santa Agathe?' Michelle asked, a hopeful note in her voice.

'Now Santa Agathe I've heard of,' Vanessa replied.

'You have?' Michelle sounded less despondent.

'There was a documentary on television recently. It's a volcanic island in the Mediterranean abandoned during a Napoleonic siege and rediscovered a hundred or so years later. It's now the playground of the rich and famous, and boasts the highest proportion of private yacht moorings in the area. How am I doing?'

'That's it,' the telephone line crackled in reply.

'So why are you so interested in Santa Agathe?'

'Haven't you been listening?' Michelle now sounded impatient.

Vanessa was occasionally guilty of tuning out when her sister called. Michelle was an avid follower of the comings and goings of the celebrity set. Vanessa wasn't quite so interested in them or their activities. Most of the people her sister referred to she had never heard of.

'I must have missed the bit about Santa Agathe,' Vanessa admitted. 'Can you run it past me again?'

'Giovanni Petucci is visiting the island for the fiesta.'

'Right,' Vanessa said, slowly taking her time. 'Fiesta?' she queried.

'Look it up.'

Vanessa sensed her sister was beginning to lose patience. 'Why?' she asked.

'Because I can't be in two places at once.'

'No, you can't,' Vanessa agreed.

'Nessa, I need your help.'

'Now why doesn't that surprise me?'

'What does that mean?' Michelle snapped.

'You've got yourself in a hole, haven't you?'

'Not really.'

'And you want me to bail you out.' Vanessa saw no reason to go easy on her sister.

'There's no need to be horrid.'

Vanessa could almost hear Michelle pouting. 'I know a tall tale when I hear one and I want the truth.'

'Didn't you say your landlord was throwing you out of your houseboat for the summer?' Michelle coaxed.

'I'm sure I didn't put it quite like that.'

'Because the roof was about to fall in?'

'I didn't say that either.' Vanessa knew she needed to focus if she was going to keep Michelle on track.

'There's sun, a yacht, all expenses

paid and we're talking bonuses too,' Michelle explained. 'What's not to like?'

'What is this all about?' Vanessa asked in a calm voice.

'I'm trying to tell you.'

'You're not making a very good job of it. Are you in trouble?'

'Course not.' Michelle's voice faded.

'Hello? Are you still there?' Vanessa called.

'Bad signal.' Michelle's voice now began to break up.

'Where exactly are you?'

'You will do it, won't you?'

'Hold on,' Vanessa stalled. 'Do what?'

'Take my place.'

'Where? Why?'

'I'll email the details. Don't let me down.'

'Michelle? Michelle?'

The line went dead. Vanessa grunted in frustration. This was so like her younger sister. She had got herself into another fix and had as usual turned to Vanessa to sort it out. Vanessa had vowed never again, after the last scrape had landed them both in a great deal of trouble. Vanessa wished her parents were here to help, but her father had been seconded to the Far East. Their mother had made Vanessa promise to keep an eye on Michelle in their absence. It was already proving a challenge.

She had thought keeping an eye on Michelle would be easy if they both worked the same cruise liners. Dancing was Michelle's life, and it had been Vanessa's until a stress fracture had invalided her out. After that, it hadn't been so easy keeping in touch with her sociable sister, who loved nothing more than taking off at a moment's notice without telling anyone where she was going.

Vanessa glanced out of the porthole of her houseboat. Rain was bouncing off the towpath with such ferocity it was hard to believe it was July. Weathermen predicted it would be the wettest summer on record, and

Vanessa believed them.

The constant drip of water leaking through a crack in the overhead canvas persuaded her that maybe a break was what she needed. Her ankle was more or less on the mend, and as long as she didn't do anything silly, a week or two in the sun could be beneficial.

Walking along the towpath to her local internet café, she ordered a latte. Then, turning on her iPad, she entered the name Giovanni Petucci into her search engine.

There was no shortage of information. According to one source, he was big on the international scene, and he and his girlfriend, the glamorous fashion icon Claudia Amoretti, were the faces of today. They were, it seemed, a modern couple whose activities featured heavily in the society columns as they jetted around the world.

Claudia was publicity advisor to a world-renowned fashion house and rubbed shoulders with the rich and famous. Giovanni was based in Turin, and was the son of a successful father who had made his money subcontracting components for the motor and aerospace industry. His mother was minor Italian aristocracy. Giovanni was their only child.

There was a photo of a confident Giovanni on board a yacht, with his arm circled around Claudia's waist. Vanessa admired her bikini-perfect figure with envy.

A few moments later, Michelle's email landed in her in box.

*   *   *

Vanessa didn't know about Giovanni Petucci being huge, but his yacht certainly was. It was moored a discreet distance off shore, but even from this distance Vanessa could see no expense had been spared. It appeared to have several decks and an outside pool. She took a few moments to admire its streamlined silhouette. Her fingertips tingled with anticipation. She missed the camaraderie of life at sea.

Following Michelle's instructions, Vanessa now texted *The Riviera* to let them know she had arrived, then she sat down under one of the parasols dotted around the private landing stage and, retrieving a small guidebook from her bag, began to read up on Santa Agathe.

The island was not big, a mere twenty kilometres long and ten kilometres wide, with a population of three thousand. Due to its location, climate and the variety of activities it could offer, it was popular with the young sun-seeking crowd and the colony of artists who inhabited the quieter inland area. Its economy relied heavily on visitors, and tourism was its gross national product.

Severino Amoretti, the renowned artist, had been born on Santa Agathe, and he rarely left the island. *Il Pomeriggio (The Afternoon)* was his world-famous masterpiece, a painting depicting his beloved wife, his muse

Maria, performing a domestic task in the afternoon sunshine. The artists who flocked to his workshop tried to copy his distinctive style, but no one could ever capture the Severino magic.

Although Severino was now widowed and lived a quiet life, there were references to him everywhere on the island. There was a Via Severino, a museum, an art gallery and a park, all named after him. Facsimiles of his flamboyant signature graced nearly every building. Only his first name was ever used, but it was instantly recognisable. He was Santa Agathe's most famous son, and the residents of Santa Agathe were justly proud of him. He was also Claudia Amoretti's father.

'Signorina Blake?'

Vanessa looked up as a tanned officer dressed in deck whites approached her. 'Yes, I am,' she greeted him with a smile.

'I am sorry to have kept you waiting,' he addressed her in perfect English, 'but if you are ready to leave, the motor launch is ready.'

Vanessa followed him, climbing down the harbour wall steps that led to the launch waiting to ferry them across to *The Riviera*. Gentle waves slapped the side of the boat. Vanessa was glad the sea was calm. Although she'd worked on cruise liners for nearly five years, she'd never really grown accustomed to the swell of water, and knew how cruel even the friendliest sea could be. As they left the harbour behind, Vanessa took a deep breath to steady her nerves.

There was no going back now, but she still couldn't shake off the feeling that something wasn't right. She'd heard nothing from Michelle since her email, and despite leaving constant voice mails, her sister had not called back. Vanessa had been in two minds about falling in with Michelle's plans, but her landlord's urgent insistence that she vacate her houseboat immediately had taken the decision out of her hands.

The launch cut its engine. 'We are

here,' the officer announced.

Vanessa gathered up her things, still wondering what her duties would be and when she would be expected to start work. She still couldn't understand why Giovanni and Claudia would need the services of a professional ballroom dancer, but over the years Vanessa had received some odd requests, and she had learned never to question any of them.

A man wearing a short-sleeved blue shirt and fitted grey trousers was waiting for her on deck. 'Michelle Grant?'

'I'm Vanessa Grant,' she explained.

'I thought your name was Michelle,' he replied.

'Michelle is my sister.'

The man frowned. 'Then what are you doing here?'

Vanessa bit down her annoyance, feeling Michelle could have at least informed Giovanni Petucci of the change of plan. 'Michelle's been unavoidably detained,' she improvised, 'and sends her apologies. I'm standing in for her.' Her smile slipped. She could see from the expression on the man's face that things weren't going well. 'Is there a problem?' she asked.

'A significant one,' he informed her tersely.

Vanessa's sense of unease deepened. 'I can prove I'm Michelle's sister, if that's what's worrying you. I have all my paperwork, and my qualifications are up to date. We were both dancing professionals employed by one of the large cruise companies, but I had to give up after I damaged my ankle.'

The man dismissed her explanation as if it were of no importance. 'Until I've done a thorough security check on you, I can't allow you to board.'

'You're not serious.' Vanessa couldn't believe what she was hearing.

'Why would I joke?'

On reflection, Vanessa could not fault his logic. She could be absolutely anybody; and in view of the yacht owner's high international profile, security concerns had to be of the greatest importance.

'But I've nowhere to go,' she protested, annoyed with herself for not having foreseen complications of this nature.

'I'm afraid that's not my problem. I do not have the authority to allow you to board.'

Used as she was to thinking on her feet, Vanessa lapsed into silence. She had downloaded a one-way air ticket, and all her other travel expenses had been charged to the Petucci account, but there had been no mention of a return flight. She was stranded.

'May I know your name?' Vanessa eventually enquired.

'Lorenzo Talbot.'

'And your position here is?'

'I'm head of security.'

'Well, Mr Talbot,' she said, glancing over her shoulder, 'I'm not a very strong swimmer; so unless you've got other ideas, you're going to have to give me permission to come aboard.'

'No one comes aboard without a security check,' he insisted.

'That may be so; but in case you haven't noticed, the launch has departed. I've no way of getting back to shore.'

Lorenzo Talbot hesitated; then, after a brief nod, he pressed the receiver on his two-way radio. Vanessa listened to a rapid exchange being conducted in a language that she couldn't follow.

'What was all that about?' she got in first as Lorenzo switched off his receiver.

'You,' was the succinct reply. 'Follow me.'

'Where are we going?'

'This way.'

'If you've any ideas of conducting a full-body search, then I should inform you that you're breaching my human rights.' Vanessa stood her ground as she addressed his broad back. Lorenzo swung round to face her with a look of surprise.

'I've no intention of touching you,' he admitted, 'or infringing your human rights.'

'I'm pleased to hear it.' Vanessa relaxed a little. At least he hadn't thrown her overboard.

'If it's not too much trouble, Ms Blake,' he said with the suggestion of a smile that totally transformed his face, 'would you mind accompanying me below deck?'

'Then I'm being given permission to board?'

'Temporarily.'

'And you're not going to lock me in chains?'

'That thought had also not occurred to me,' he replied, opening a door and indicating that she should go through.

Left with no choice but to follow, Vanessa picked up her bag, deciding that the next time she met up with her sister, there would be a blunt exchange of home truths.

2

'Make yourself comfortable.' Lorenzo indicated a crew seat in a corner of the cramped cabin. 'I'm sorry there isn't much room,' he apologised.

Vanessa managed to squeeze into the only available space. Then, deciding she had been outspoken enough for one day, she waited for Lorenzo to dictate the pace. She closed her eyes. The background hum of mechanism and constant flashing lights in the control room were beginning to give her a headache.

She had barely slept or eaten properly over the past twenty-four hours, and the lack of nourishment was beginning to catch up with her. She was also worried about Michelle. Where was she, and why wasn't she answering her calls? She was guilty of doing some pretty crazy things in the past, but this latest escapade was extreme even by her standards.

'Do you know my sister?' Vanessa asked as Lorenzo showed no inclination to break the silence that had fallen between them.

'I've never met her.' Lorenzo carried on tapping his keyboard.

'Then who did her security checks?'

'One of my colleagues.'

'If your security is so good, how did I manage to travel all the way from Gatwick on her ticket?' Vanessa bit her lip. So much for her resolution to keep quiet.

'The ticket was open,' Lorenzo replied. 'But it's a good point. One I shall take up with my colleague. Thank you for raising it.' He threw her a brief smile.

'Don't mention it.' Vanessa stifled a yawn, fatigue getting the better of her.

'Would you like a cup of coffee?' she heard Lorenzo ask through closed eyes.

'Mm,' she answered, before realising she was in danger of falling asleep.

'Sorry.' She stifled another yawn behind the back of her hand.

'Wait here,' Lorenzo instructed.

Vanessa glanced across to his workstation, wondering if she could sneak a look at Michelle's credentials while he was getting the coffee.

'Everything's password encoded, so don't even think about it.' Lorenzo paused in the doorway, having accurately read her mind.

Vanessa flushed. 'A cup of coffee would be lovely. Thank you,' she mumbled.

Lorenzo was back moments later with a loaded tray. 'I know it's the wrong time of day for breakfast, but would you like one?'

Vanessa had to restrain her impulse to attack a couple of the fluffy golden croissants before Lorenzo had properly settled down again. 'Delicious,' she mumbled as the pastry melted in her mouth.

'Glad to hear I've got something right,' was Lorenzo's wry response.

'Have another one.' He proffered the basket and nudged some cherry jam in her direction. 'Local delicacy.'

'I shouldn't, really.' Vanessa did her best to resist, her fingers hovering over the butter dish.

'Don't mind me.' Lorenzo turned his attention back to his computer screen.

Vanessa frowned, not sure what to make of him. His swept-back dark hair and first name suggested Mediterranean parentage, yet he spoke faultless English, and Talbot sounded decidedly Anglo-Saxon. She inhaled the fragrance of fresh coffee before taking an appreciative sip. Already she was beginning to feel better.

Looking up from his keyboard, Lorenzo asked, 'Where's Mr Vargas?'

'Who?' Vanessa asked with a perplexed frown, putting down her cup.

'Your dancing partner.'

'I don't have one.'

'It says here you do, or rather your sister does.'

'My sister didn't say anything about a

dancing partner.'

'Paolo Vargas?' Lorenzo prompted.

'I've never heard of him.'

'I would very much like to speak to your sister,' Lorenzo said.

'That makes two of us.'

'Do you know where she is?'

Vanessa hesitated. 'I'm trying to get in touch with her,' she replied, reluctant to admit she had no idea of her sister's whereabouts.

'May I see your passport, please?' Lorenzo asked.

She handed it over, her annoyance increasing by the second. She never told tales on her sister, but although she didn't want to worry them, their parents would have to be informed of this latest development if Michelle didn't contact her soon.

'Vanessa Blake.' Lorenzo spelled out her name, looking up at her for confirmation.

Vanessa nodded, holding her breath as he tapped out her name, wondering exactly what information his search engine would reveal.

'Have you found me?' she asked when she was unable to bear the silence any longer.

'Yes.'

'And?'

'Your name comes up,' Lorenzo said with a frown, 'as an associate of someone called Charlie Hooper?'

Vanessa's mouth went dry. 'Charlie Hooper?' she managed to croak. The swell of the yacht and her recently consumed croissants were now beginning to make her feel sick.

'Is he someone else you've never heard of?'

'No, the name is familiar to me,' Vanessa admitted.

'Are you going to tell me about him?'

'Charlie Hooper was years ago.'

'It says here you were involved with him.'

'I wasn't. Well I was, but I was a teenager. We were part of a gang. He was the leader and he went around doing things.'

'Making trouble, you mean.'

Vanessa squirmed. 'I was only involved in a minor disturbance in the municipal fountain. We'd been to a party and someone jumped in, and we all sort of followed.'

'I see the police were called.'

'It was a case of high spirits, that's all.'

'High spirits that got out of hand?'

'Surely an innocent bit of a fun doesn't constitute a police record?'

'Not for you maybe, but your Charlie Hooper went seriously off the rails after that incident.'

'He wasn't my Charlie Hooper, and I haven't seen him for years.'

'Haven't you?'

'When my parents discovered what was going on, they put a stop to the relationship.'

'What exactly was going on?'

Vanessa blushed with mortification as she remembered her adolescent crush on the neighbourhood bad boy and how she'd accused her mother of not understanding true love. Now with the wisdom of her twenty-five years, she realised her mother had been right, and she was truly grateful she had been sent away to stay with an aunt in Cornwall before any serious damage was done. After a summer spent enjoying long healthy walks, eating good home-cooked food and indulging in water sports, she had worked Charlie Hooper out of her system. Today was the first time she had thought about him in years.

'Nothing happened.'

'I'm pleased to hear it. Is there anything else in your past I should know about?' Lorenzo asked.

Vanessa shook her head. Her stomach was now churning so badly she didn't care about the job any more. She just wanted to get off the yacht, find Michelle and throttle her.

'Do you have any health issues?'

'I sustained a stress fracture to my ankle, and it plays up now and then. That's why I gave up dancing. I also suffer from mild sea sickness.'

Lorenzo produced a flip chart and ticked a few boxes on the form in front of him.

'Have I got the job?' Vanessa asked, wondering if he'd had a change of heart.

'No.'

'Then what's with the past boy-friends and my health history?'

'Mr Petucci is very strict about security.'

'I know, but you still haven't answered my question.'

'If — and it's a big if — you were allowed to stay on board, there would be stringent procedures that would need to be carried out, and I am not going to have time to go through them all.'

'Then you're stuck, aren't you?' She began to gain confidence. 'No Michelle and no dancing partner.'

'It's a minor setback.'

'What are you going to do?'

'I have the final say on Mr Petucci's

security, so if you're harbouring any other secrets, you'd better tell me about them now.'

'Why? You've just told me I haven't got the job.'

'I could be persuaded to change my mind.'

'Like heck you could. If you think I'm in the market for buying favours, then I have to tell you I'm not that desperate.'

'Now what are you talking about?'

Vanessa wasn't entirely sure, but she knew how important it was to maintain a confident profile in these types of situations. 'I don't do bribes, but I suppose it's a way of life to some people.'

'I'm not suggesting anything of the sort.' Lorenzo ran a hand through his hair. 'Are you always this impossible?' He held up a hand. 'No — don't answer that question.'

'Perhaps if I could have a word with Mr Petucci?' Vanessa did her best to sound reasonable, fearing she might have gone too far with her last remark.

'No you could not,' was the clipped response.

She tossed back her head. 'Then as I appear to have fallen at the first hurdle, you'd better call that launch thing back, and I'll be on my way. I'm sorry to have bothered you.'

'You can't leave.'

'And you can't hold me here against my will.'

'You're right. I can't.'

'Neither can you make me walk the plank. I told you, I'm a poor swimmer.'

'You can't leave because we've drawn anchor.'

As if to endorse this statement, there was a deep rumble somewhere below Vanessa's feet. 'We've done what?' she asked in a faint voice, her newfound confidence evaporating.

'Didn't you notice?'

Vanessa now realised it was the swell of the yacht putting out to sea that had been making her feel sick and not her snack of coffee and croissants. 'Where are we going?' she asked.

'I'm afraid I cannot reveal our destination.'

'Now who's being impossible?'

Lorenzo's lips twitched. He looked as though he didn't really want to smile but couldn't help himself. 'I can't tell you where we are going because I don't actually know.'

'Then doesn't Mr Petucci have a helicopter or something?'

Lorenzo raised an eyebrow. 'You can fly a helicopter?'

'What I mean is, don't these millionaires have things like that on board in case there's an emergency and someone has to leave in a hurry?'

'The last time I looked, there was no helicopter on deck,' Lorenzo said, the teasing note still in his voice. 'And to put you right on one thing . . . ' He paused. ' . . . it is Mr Petucci's father Enrico who owns the yacht.'

'That's all very interesting,' she said dismissively, 'but where does it leave me?'

Lorenzo handed back her passport. 'Your sister was employed to act as dance hostess for the weekend.'

'Only for the weekend?' Vanessa repeated.

'Were you expecting something longer?'

'Michelle said . . . ' Vanessa ground to a halt as she tried to recall her sister's words.

'Yes?' Lorenzo prompted.

'I thought the booking was for longer than two days.'

'Mr Petucci has planned a mini-cruise around the archipelago with a few carefully chosen guests. They will board later today after we have made our first stop.'

'Perhaps I could disembark at one of the outlying islands.'

'You could, but there is no transport back to the mainland.'

'Not from any of them?'

Lorenzo shook his head.

'Then how did these guests get there?'

'By private charter.'

Vanessa leaned forward. 'Couldn't I hitch a lift? Someone's bound to have a spare seat on a pedalo or something.'

'Not without the relevant security clearance.'

'Which I haven't got.'

'At last we seem to be speaking the same language.'

The engine continued its rhythmic chug.

'You mentioned you could be persuaded to change your mind?' Vanessa spoke slowly.

'I do have an idea.'

'Why don't you run it past me?' Vanessa encouraged, 'and see if I like it?'

'Mr Petucci planned a dancing display to start the evening off, and that's why your sister was booked. Agreed?'

'If you say so. You're the one with all the answers.'

'You can dance?'

Vanessa nodded, thinking of the

sequinned dress she had packed only the day before. It was a shame it wouldn't see the light of day. Turquoise was her favourite colour. The Spanish seamstress on her last cruise had made it especially for her, saying turquoise brought out the colour in her eyes.

'Yes, I can dance,' she replied. 'In fact, I'm more highly qualified than Michelle.'

'Your sister has full security clearance.' Lorenzo raised his eyebrows. 'So if you were amenable, we could work something out, if you get my drift?'

The truth began to dawn on Vanessa.

'Would you be prepared to assume a temporary change of identity?'

'You want me to pretend to be my sister for the weekend?'

'Have you any objection?'

'That's fraud, isn't it?'

'I'm not technically sure of the correct term, but as long as you give me your promise that you don't intend to infringe any onboard regulations, I'm prepared to sanction the identity swap.'

'Can you do that?'

'I have the necessary authority.'

'Supposing someone recognises me? Mediterranean cruising is a small world.'

'That's a risk we are going to have to take.' Lorenzo passed over a sheet of paper. 'Do you recognise any of these names?'

'Who are they?'

'The guests who will be attending tonight's party.'

Vanessa cast an eye down the list. 'None of them look familiar to me.'

'Then will you do it?'

'What happens if I say no?'

'You're free to disembark at our first stop.'

'You said there was no transport.'

'I'm sure someone like you could work something out.'

'You wouldn't dare dump me.'

'You are on board without the captain's permission, and as there's no record of you having embarked, no one will miss you.'

'Yes there is. I was picked up by motor launch, and the officer addressed me as Ms Blake.'

'Ms Michelle Blake?'

Vanessa opened her mouth to protest, but knew further argument would only result in an undignified scene. Lorenzo held all the aces, and he knew it.

'Two people can play dirty,' she said, drawing on the iron reserve that had got her through various past crises in her life. It was time to call Lorenzo's bluff. 'I'll do it, on one condition.'

'You are in no position to bargain.'

'Neither are you, Mr Talbot. I'm sure you wouldn't want Mr Petucci to discover you'd failed in your duties as chief security officer and weren't above practising a little bribery. You could be facing a sudden and unexpected career change.'

Vanessa felt a small thrill of satisfaction as, with a wary look in his eyes, Lorenzo enquired, 'What is this condition?'

'Can you dance?'

'I beg your pardon?'

'The tango?' Vanessa added out of a sense of devilment. 'You're the right height and build, and I can't do a display on my own, and I doubt Mr Vargas will put in a late appearance.'

'I'm sure we can find a member of the crew willing to volunteer to do the honours.'

'I want you as my partner, and if you don't agree then the deal is off.'

3

Vanessa wasn't proud of the challenge she had laid down. It had been an ill-disciplined thing to do; but Lorenzo Talbot needed taking down a peg or two. He was acting as if this whole situation was her fault.

She waited with bated breath for his reaction, and had difficulty containing her gasp of surprise when he said, 'If it's the only solution, then yes, I can tango.'

'You'll do it?'

'Haven't I just said so?'

'But did you mean it?'

'There's a crew briefing six o'clock tonight in the ballroom. Don't be late.'

'What about a rehearsal?' Vanessa began to fear that yet again her tongue had got her into trouble.

'I'll sort something out. It's this way.'

Vanessa began to gather up her

things as Lorenzo opened the door to the cabin, letting in a welcome draught of fresh air.

'I suggest you get some rest. Mr Petucci rarely retires before midnight, and the staff have to stay on duty until after he has gone to bed.'

Vanessa followed Lorenzo down to a lower deck, wondering if she would ever find her way back up to the ballroom. A security light came on as they stopped outside a door at the end of a dark passage.

'If you want anything,' Lorenzo said, indicating a bell push on the wall, 'you can summon one of the stewards.'

The cabin was surprisingly roomy. Vanessa quickly unpacked her treasured sequinned dress and hung it up to let any creases fall out. Then, after refreshing herself in the small shower, she stretched out on her bunk and promptly fell asleep. To her horror, she didn't wake up until half past five. Knowing how long it would take to prepare herself for the evening ahead, she dressed more hurriedly than she would have wished, aware that due to her sedentary lifestyle, she had gained a few pounds since she had been measured for her dress. Emerging from the cabin with only five minutes to spare, she accosted a passing steward, who greeted her with a friendly smile.

'The ballroom? I will take you, signorina. It is not easy to find when you are new, and Mr Talbot would not like you to be late. My name is Lizabetta.'

'I'm . . . ' Vanessa paused. ' . . . Michelle,' she said and held out her hand, hoping she didn't look too guilty about the subterfuge.

'Welcome to *The Riviera*, Michelle. I hope you will be happy here.'

'Thank you.'

'That is a lovely dress. I wish I was as slim as you, but I eat too much ice-cream. Here we are.' Lizabetta paused outside a set of double doors. 'We've made it with two minutes to spare.'

Vanessa could hear the murmur of voices. Taking a deep breath, she pushed open one of the doors. The ballroom fell silent. All eyes turned in her direction. She faltered in the doorway before feeling a sharp nudge in the ribs.

'You're late.'

She spun round. Lorenzo Talbot was standing behind her, dressed in white tie and tails.

'I . . . I'm punctual,' she stuttered, unable to believe the transformation from security officer to drop-dead gorgeous dancing professional. 'I got here before you.'

'You cut it fine.'

I fell asleep,' she admitted, 'and didn't realise the time.'

'Well now you are here, would you mind introducing yourself to everyone, Michelle?' There was a guarded warning in Lorenzo's eyes as he emphasised her name.

Vanessa blinked, then nodded and made her way to the centre of the room.

'Off you go,' Lorenzo encouraged her.

A smattering of applause broke out as Vanessa took the stand. 'Hi, my name is Michelle Blake,' she began. 'I'll be doing the dancing display.' She looked round at the sea of interested faces and fell back on her old standby. 'Does anyone have any questions?'

'Isn't Mr Talbot a little overdressed for a briefing session?' a grinning steward enquired.

'Mr Talbot has kindly agreed to stand in for Mr Vargas, my dancing partner, who has been unavoidably delayed.'

'Good on you, mate.' The Australian voice now sounded friendly, and Vanessa began to relax. 'I can't dance, but if you're ever looking for a surfing partner, Michelle, I'm your man. Kyle Andrews, address Bondi Beach.'

'I'll bear that in mind.' Vanessa smiled at Kyle. 'And thank you for the warm welcome. I'll do my best to be a good member of the team.'

'In that dress you can't fail,' one of

the female security guards added. 'Don't put it in the laundry bin, otherwise I'll have it off you.'

Lorenzo strode to the middle of the room. 'If you wouldn't mind taking a seat, Ms Blake, we'll get on with the briefing.'

The briefing was followed by a buffet snack the chef had provided to sustain the crew throughout the evening.

'Sorry,' Lorenzo apologised, only pausing to snatch up a sandwich, 'we're only going to have time for a short rehearsal. This afternoon's activities have completely thrown my schedule and I'm way behind with everything.'

'I downloaded some suitable music a while ago,' Vanessa said, clicking on the app on her phone.

'Then let's go for it.'

As the crew dispersed, Lorenzo led her onto the intimate dance floor. Vanessa did her best to concentrate as he put a firm hand around her waist. Slowly they began to practise the intricate manoeuvres required to execute a polished performance of the tango. With his face only inches from hers, Vanessa inhaled his citrus aftershave and tried to focus on her dance steps and not the way his body moved in perfect sync with the music. As the tempo increased, she arched her back. All that was stopping her from falling to the floor was Lorenzo's hand supporting the small of her back. She tried not to tense and to let her body sway with the music. The tango was an instinctive dance, and to be a success it had to speak for itself.

As the music rose to its final crescendo, Lorenzo whirled her round and crushed her body to his in one fluid movement that took her breath away.

'How did I do?' he asked as the ballroom fell silent.

'You're good,' Vanessa acknowledged, hoping she wasn't breathing too heavily.

'In that case, I'll see you later.'

His departure was followed by a slow handclap.

'Wow, you sure set the floor alight.'

Kyle was grinning at her. 'I always took Lorenzo for stuffy. Guess I'm going to have to have a rethink.'

'I, um . . . ' Vanessa put a hand to her face. ' . . . think I'll get some air.'

'Good on you.'

Kyle's friendly voice rang in her ears as Vanessa made her way to the upper deck. With her hand resting on the railing, she steadied her breathing while her pulse and heartbeat returned to normal. She tried to convince herself that her body had forgotten the discipline of dance and that her heightened emotions were nothing to do with the way Lorenzo Talbot executed the tango.

She knew from her studies that the tango had been introduced into South American dance halls for the sailors who, back on land after months at sea, needed to refresh their dancing skills. Lorenzo's dancing skills needed no such refreshing.

Hearing movements behind her, Vanessa turned and, smiling at a couple of Mr Petucci's guests who like her were enjoying the evening air, she made her way back into the ballroom.

'There's no need to be nervous,' Lorenzo said as they waited for the guests to settle down before they started their display.

'I'm not,' Vanessa insisted.

'Kyle said something about you looking a tad overheated earlier.'

Before Vanessa could reply, there was a loud drum roll and a clash of cymbals. The lights were lowered. The compère stepped onto the stage and began his introduction.

'Ladies and gentlemen, tonight we have a special treat for you. The world-renowned Michelle Blake has managed to find a gap in her busy schedule and has graciously agreed to perform for us tonight.'

'World-renowned?' Vanessa cast Lorenzo a horrified glance. 'Busy schedule?'

The spotlight cast an amber glow on the dance floor as Lorenzo squeezed her fingers. 'I had no idea you were famous,' he said.

'Neither did I.' Vanessa wasn't sure if her fingertips tingled from the touch of Lorenzo's fingers on hers or his devastating smile.

'Partnering her for the very first time — ' The compère cast Lorenzo an encouraging look. ' — is our very own Lorenzo Talbot.'

The guests broke into polite applause.

'We're on,' Lorenzo said. He swept her onto the dance floor. 'Terrific dress,' he whispered in her ear as they waited for the music to start.

Swinging into their routine for a second time, Vanessa's experience told her that the chemistry between them was creating a special kind of magic. It happened with some partners, and this was one of those occasions. She could feel Lorenzo's muscles against hers as he eased the pressure off her ankle, allowing her concentrate on the intricate fluid body movements the tango demanded.

They took their bows to rapturous applause from the guests and crew.

'Where did you learn to dance like that?' Vanessa asked in the rest room as they retreated to take a well-earned break.

'I have two sisters.' Lorenzo poured out some fresh fruit juice. 'They liked to dance. As I am their only brother, I was in constant demand.' He eased his tie away from his collar and sat down opposite her. 'The skills my sisters taught me have proved useful for social occasions, and it helps to keep me fit. I used to go to the gym but I had to give it up.'

'Why?' Vanessa asked, intrigued.

'Like you, I have an injury.'

'You should have said.' A pang of guilt tugged at Vanessa's conscience. 'What happened?'

'I hurt my shoulders.'

'What were you doing?'

'Chasing someone.'

His pager bleeped. Lorenzo glanced down at the flashing red light.

'I need to see to this. Take your time. There's no need to rush back to the ballroom.'

At the end of a surprisingly pleasant evening chatting to the guests, Vanessa strolled onto the deck. Harbour lights twinkled in the distance and the moon cast silver shadows on the water. She wondered about their exact location. *The Riviera* had moored several hours ago, but no one on the crew seemed to know on which island.

'Mr Petucci takes his privacy right seriously,' Kyle Andrews informed her. 'Best not ask too many questions. He doesn't like that sort of thing.'

As Vanessa gazed into the inky darkness, the smell of sulphur from the distant hot springs mingled with the background chatter of the sophisticated guests enjoying their evening's entertainment. Her attention was alerted to the sound of a soft footfall.

'Good evening, Miss Blake.'

She gripped the handrail, not daring to turn round. The man spoke with an easy familiarity that suggested he might be a friend of Michelle's.

'I was sorry to have missed your performance tonight. My guests tell me it was knockout. Unfortunately, family business delayed me in Turin. My father had matters for me to attend to, but now the weekend is ours.'

Vanessa turned round very slowly. The man was dressed in a grey suit with a discreet blue tie and business shirt.

'Giovanni Petucci at your service.'

He kissed her hand. Giovanni was younger than Vanessa had envisaged, but he looked every inch the urbane professional. 'I may call you Michelle?' he asked.

'Of course.' Vanessa relaxed. Giovanni Petucci had not recognised her. 'Is Miss Amoretti with you?' she asked, feeling the tension ease from the back of her neck.

'Tomorrow. She arrives tomorrow.' Giovanni's slow smile was beginning to make Vanessa feel uncomfortable. 'So the night is ours.'

'It's a pleasure to meet you, Mr Petucci.'

'Giovanni, please,' he insisted. 'You are shivering. Are you cold?'

'A little.'

'That dress does not provide much protection against a chill breeze.' His eyes travelled over her bare shoulders.

'Perhaps I had better return to the ballroom.'

'I have a better idea.' Giovanni blocked her way. 'Why don't you warm up with a nightcap in my suite?'

'That's very kind of you,' Vanessa said, playing for time, 'but I wouldn't want to put you to any bother.'

'I have to get out of these clothes. They are hot and uncomfortable, not at all suitable for a cruise.'

'I need to fetch a wrap from my cabin.'

'Send one of the stewards.' Giovanni's eyes narrowed. 'My suite is this way.'

'I promised to partner one of your

guests in a dance.' Vanessa didn't like the idea of being alone with Giovanni.

His eyes hardened. 'I do not allow my wishes to be countermanded by members of my crew.'

Vanessa began to regret having left the ballroom.

'And I'm sure you wouldn't want me to tell my father that your behaviour had been less than sociable?'

'No, of course not. But your guests — ?'

'Can entertain themselves.' Placing a firm hand around her waist, Giovanni began to urge Vanessa towards the upper deck. In the distance, a shadow moved. Startled, Vanessa stumbled against Giovanni, forcing him to tighten his hold.

'That's more like it.' Giovanni's low laugh sent a shudder up her backbone. 'It's this way.'

4

'Mr Petucci.'

The shadow materialised out of the darkness, and Vanessa grabbed her chance to move away from Giovanni's unwelcome intimacy. Lorenzo had changed from his white tie and tails back into his security uniform, and now stood respectfully to one side, waiting for Giovanni to acknowledge his presence.

'What is it?' Giovanni snapped. 'I'm busy.'

'A message has just come through for you.'

'Can't you deal with it?'

'It's Miss Amoretti.'

Muttering under his breath, Giovanni strode away in the direction of the radio control room. Lorenzo turned his attention to Vanessa.

'Mr Petucci and I were talking,' she

began to explain.

'I saw you,' Lorenzo replied, 'and it looked like you were doing a lot more than talking.'

Vanessa flushed. 'It's not what it seems.'

'It never is.'

'What's that supposed to mean?' Vanessa flared up.

'Exactly what I say.' Lorenzo paused, adding, 'Mr Petucci is a difficult man to refuse.'

Vanessa knew she was being ungracious. 'Thank you for coming to my rescue,' she said in a quieter tone of voice.

'Don't mention it.'

'It's fortunate Miss Amoretti chose that moment to call.'

'I may have overemphasised the call's importance,' Lorenzo confessed.

'Miss Amoretti didn't want to speak to Giovanni?'

'I could have taken a message, but let's not talk about them.' Lorenzo placed a hand under Vanessa's elbow.

'What are you doing?' Vanessa, still twitchy from Giovanni's unwelcome attention, tried without success to wriggle free.

'Getting you away from here as soon as possible.'

'We've already had this conversation. I thought we'd agreed you can't dump me on an island where the only mode of transport would appear to be by donkey.'

'I haven't time to argue with you. We need to get off the deck and back to the ballroom right now.'

The tone of Lorenzo's voice alarmed Vanessa. She looked round in concern. 'Are we in danger?'

'Of a sort. Mr Petucci doesn't like having his plans upset. Out here on deck, you are at his mercy, but he wouldn't dare insist you join him for a private nightcap in front of his guests. Several of them are friends of his father's.'

'But he and Claudia Amoretti are an item.'

'That's why he needed to take that call.'

'Couldn't his behaviour be classed as harassment?'

'Harassment or not, on board *The Riviera* Giovanni calls the shots; and if you should happen to turn down his invitation, he wouldn't hesitate to dump you among the donkeys.'

'You're not serious.'

'Never more so. We also don't want him discovering your true identity, so I suggest you keep out of Giovanni's way for the remainder of your stay.'

'How am I going to do that?'

'There are several excursions planned for tomorrow.'

'Surely they're for guests only?'

'Agreed, but until they return most of the crew will be off duty, so why don't we grab a picnic and take off for one of the white sand beaches?'

'Supposing Giovanni has the same idea?'

'The sea beds around here are teeming with marine biology. He is keen on water sports, and Kyle Andrews has arranged to take some of the younger set driving. He'll probably join them, or go windsurfing.'

'But if he decides to stay on board, won't you have to stay as well?'

'I can arrange cover.'

'Why are you doing this for me?' Vanessa was forced to ask.

'Would it make you feel any better if I said it was to keep you from poking around my records?'

'You still don't trust me, do you?'

The faint sound of footsteps further along the deck forestalled Lorenzo's reply. 'We'd better get going,' he urged.

Back in the ballroom, the sound of a trio of musicians playing toe-tapping show numbers greeted them.

'I've been looking for you every-where,' a male guest accosted Vanessa. 'You promised me a dance.'

'I did indeed.' Vanessa put on her best professional smile. 'Do you tango, or something a little less energetic?'

'I'll leave you to it,' Lorenzo murmured in her ear. 'Make sure someone escorts you back to your cabin, and I'll see you in the morning.'

★ ★ ★

After breakfast and the departure of the guests to enjoy their day's activities, Lorenzo informed the crew they were free to do as they wished until late afternoon.

'I've got you one of these.' He produced a backpack and gave it to Vanessa. 'Best stock up.'

'With what?'

He reeled off a list: 'Sunscreen, water, swimsuit, towels, mosquito repellent. And bring your passport.'

'We're only going for the morning, aren't we?'

'We don't want anyone finding out you aren't really Michelle Blake. Meet me back here in . . . ' He glanced at his watch. ' . . . a quarter of an hour?'

'Where's Giovanni?' Vanessa couldn't

shake off the feeling that he might suddenly appear and demand she join him for the day.

'We're in luck. One of the guests has arranged a diving competition, and as Giovanni loves a challenge, he's gone off with them.'

Down in her cabin, Vanessa changed into a pair of pink Capri pants and a cool cotton top; then, securing her shoulder-length blonde hair into a scrunchie, she thrust it under a straw hat before hurrying to the upper deck, where Lorenzo was waiting for her. He too had changed into cut-off cargo pants and sleeveless T-shirt.

'Ready?' he asked.

She nodded, doing her best to remind herself that this date was no more than a business meeting in somewhat unusual circumstances and with an alternative dress code. Out of his uniform, Lorenzo looked ready for the beach, and she realised his tanned limbs could prove a serious distraction to the seriousness of the situation. She was on a yacht under false pretences, masquerading as her sister and about to go off on a picnic with the head of security. She doubted their circumstances would stand up well under investigation.

'You're absolutely sure about this?' Vanessa decided to give Lorenzo one last chance to back out.

'As long as you're not scared of frogs, big painted ones with bulging eyes. They are quite harmless really, but on first sight they can be rather startling.'

'I mean, supposing something unforeseen happens.'

'You worry too much,' Lorenzo chided.

'With good cause.'

'Nothing's going to go wrong,' he assured her. 'So come on, before the launch leaves without us.'

* * *

Vanessa inspected the handlebars and tested the brakes of an antiquated

56

bicycle as Lorenzo handed over payment to the proprietor of the small hire shop.

'Is this all they've got?' she asked.

'It's either that or a donkey.'

Vanessa settled onto the saddle and performed a few experimental turns of the pedals. They made an interesting noise, but she was relieved to see they didn't fall off.

'Ready?'

'As ready as I'll ever be,' Vanessa replied.

'Watch out for potholes,' Lorenzo warned.

The path down to the cove was rocky and required every ounce of Vanessa's concentration. Lorenzo kept up a steady rate, and Vanessa pedalled valiantly after him, glad she had worn sensible deck shoes and not a flimsy pair of flip-flops. More than once she lost her footing on the pedals and, unused to such intense physical activity, her calf muscles began to cramp. Vanessa's level of fitness had dipped since her dancing days, and gentle cycling along a friendly towpath was a completely different experience to the challenging terrain of a volcanic island.

In any other circumstances, she would have enjoyed the heady smell of pine trees and the brief glimpse of a golden butterfly as it landed on a clump of pink spiked thistle. The azure sea sparkled invitingly in the morning sunshine. But the pace was too punishing for Vanessa to do more than merely register she was cycling through one of the world's most beautiful nature reserves.

Just as she was beginning to think she could go no further, Lorenzo signalled to the right. The welcoming shade provided a brief respite from the relentless sun, even if the bumpy ride was now worse than the coastal sandy path. The vegetation gave way to a clearing, and below them Vanessa caught sight of a secluded cove.

'We'll have to leave the bikes up here.' Lorenzo dismounted, looking infuriatingly fresh. 'Hardly anyone comes this way, so they'll be quite safe if we put them under the bushes. Got everything you need?'

Vanessa nodded.

'Then down we go. Can you manage, or do you want a hand?'

'I'm fine,' Vanessa insisted.

'You need to watch your footing,' Lorenzo advised.

Vanessa scrambled down the cliff path, Lorenzo leading the way. 'It's breathtaking,' she gasped as she landed on the sand, at last able to appreciate her magical surroundings.

'I come here whenever I can,' Lorenzo admitted, 'which isn't often enough. Over there I think.' Lorenzo indicated a secluded corner of the cove, and they began to trudge towards the sheltered spot he had chosen. 'This should do.'

Vanessa kicked off her deck shoes. The sand was hot underneath the soles of her feet.

'Better put some towels down,' Lorenzo

advised. 'You never know what's crawling over the sand.' He handed Vanessa a water bottle, then delved into his rucksack. 'I missed out on breakfast, and cycling always gives me an appetite.' He began unloading some packages. 'We've got fruit, ham, tomatoes, croissants, lemon blossom honey, and the chef's speciality — marzipan fruits.'

Vanessa nibbled on some plump purple grapes and took a few moments out to watch Lorenzo as he unpacked his rucksack.

'You're looking at me,' he said, causing her to blush.

'I was wondering about you,' she admitted, swallowing some water.

'You were?' His task finished, he looked up at her.

'Lorenzo is an Italian name, but Talbot sounds English.'

'I'm named after my grandfather. He was called Lorenzo. My mother was of Italian descent. My father came from Norfolk. Does that satisfy your curiosity?'

'I just wondered, that's all.' Vanessa lowered her eyes from Lorenzo's searching gaze, wishing he didn't have the power to make her feel so uncomfortable.

'That's OK.' He smiled. 'You've given me the perfect excuse to ask you about your sister.'

Vanessa began to peel a tangerine. 'There's not much to tell, really. We spent a lot of time growing up on our grandparents' farm because our parents were often away.' The sunshine began to ease her tension. She popped a piece of tangerine into her mouth, welcoming its bitter tang. 'You wouldn't suspect I know how to milk a cow, would you?'

'Nothing about you would surprise me,' Lorenzo admitted.

Vanessa squeezed some pips out of another segment of tangerine. 'Michelle was the scatty one. I was the sensible older sister.'

'Apart from your fling with Charlie Hooper?'

Vanessa went on the offensive. 'That

was a teenage blip. Didn't you have one?'

'I used to ride a motorbike much too fast, but then I fell off and I had to sell it because I couldn't afford to get it repaired. Just as well, really. I was a menace in leathers and a crash helmet. I even had my kit painted with go-faster stripes.'

The thought of Lorenzo in black leathers astride a motorbike conjured up images that sent Vanessa's imagination into overdrive. Apart from Charlie Hooper, there hadn't been much time for men in her life. Working unsocial hours coupled with long tours of duty aboard cruise liners were a death-knell to any potential relationship.

'Do you feel like a swim before we get serious about the picnic?' The sound of Lorenzo's voice drew Vanessa out of her daydream. 'You can strip off behind that rock.'

Vanessa emerged a few minutes later in her black one-piece swimsuit.

'Race you,' Lorenzo called out, then

took off across the sand with Vanessa laughing in hot pursuit.

The sea was velvet-soft. While Lorenzo struck out towards a small outcrop of rocks, Vanessa splashed around in the shallower waters and floated on her back, looking up at the carpet of blue sky overhead. By the time she towelled herself dry, she was beginning to believe that Lorenzo was right and that she had been worrying unnecessarily about the strange situation she was in.

'Try one of these.' Lorenzo held up a plate of tempting pastries.

'I don't think I should,' Vanessa declined his offer with a sigh. 'I have to get into my sparkly dress again tonight.'

'Perhaps you're right,' Lorenzo agreed. 'I almost split my jacket last night, and we don't want you ruining your green dress.'

'Turquoise,' Vanessa corrected him.

'Turquoise,' Lorenzo repeated slowly. 'The colour of mermaids.' He began repacking the remains of their picnic and missed Vanessa's heightened colour. She'd never thought of herself as a mermaid.

'I'd better change back into my clothes,' she mumbled, not looking at him.

'Finished?' he asked as Vanessa emerged from behind her rock suitably clad for the return journey.

She squeezed the seawater out of her swimsuit and towelled her hair dry. 'Think so,' she replied, flicking the last drops of moisture from her eyelids.

'*Le isole di magia*,' Lorenzo said slowly.

'What does that mean?' Vanessa asked.

'The islands of magic. That's what the locals call the archipelago, and I think they've worked their magic on you.'

Vanessa suspected the warm feeling that crept up her spine was nothing to do with island magic or the summer sunshine. 'Exactly how many females have you seduced with that line?' she said, thrusting her swimsuit into her backpack.

'You're the first,' he replied.

Vanessa bit her tongue, sorely tempted to say she didn't believe him.

'Is that the time?' Lorenzo pulled his watch out of a side pocket of his rucksack. 'Hurry up or we'll miss the launch.'

It was waiting for them by the time they tumbled into it after a frantic pedal back to the bicycle shop. The skipper grinned at their suntanned faces.

'No need to rush. We've one more passenger to come,' he announced.

Lorenzo looked at him in surprise. 'Who?'

'One of the private charter people.'

'But this is the crew launch.'

'I know, but it's the last one of the day. She had no choice, but she's not very pleased about it, I can tell you.'

'She?' Vanessa echoed, ignoring the thud of her heartbeat in her chest.

'Miss Amoretti — and there she is now.'

5

The short trip back to *The Riviera* was conducted in silence. Vanessa had made a move to introduce herself to Giovanni's girlfriend, but Lorenzo had frowned and put out a hand to restrain her.

Claudia was wearing the uniform of understated chic — a plain white T-shirt, bright orange jacket and cream jeans. It was easy enough to avoid eye contact, as she did not remove her designer dark glasses, preferring instead to scroll through her incoming texts.

Their launch bumped against the side of *The Riviera*, and Lorenzo and Vanessa waited respectfully while Claudia boarded the yacht first.

'Why do I get the feeling she disapproves of me?' Vanessa asked Lorenzo in a quiet voice when Claudia was out of hearing.

'I don't think it's anything personal,' Lorenzo assured her. 'And don't forget,' he added as he helped her onto the deck, 'you're Michelle from now on in.'

As soon as she descended to her cabin, Vanessa detected a change in atmosphere. 'What's going on?' she asked Lizabetta, who was ready to scurry past without a word.

'Miss Amoretti is due on board.'

'She's already here. We travelled back with her on the crew launch.'

Lizabetta gave an agitated squeak. 'I have been assigned to her cabin. I am so nervous I keep dropping things. Do you have everything you need? I may not be around later.'

'Don't worry about me,' Vanessa assured her. 'You carry on. I can manage.'

Although she would have liked a rest before the start of her evening shift, by the time Vanessa had showered and washed the salt water out of her hair she had less than half an hour to get ready for the six o'clock briefing. There was a sense of urgency in the air as she headed towards the ballroom.

Kyle Andrews caught up with her. 'We're not in there tonight. It's out of bounds.'

'Is something special happening?'

'You must be the only person on board who hasn't heard. They're getting engaged.'

'Who?'

'Mr Petucci and Ms Amoretti, that's who. He's got her a special ring. It used to belong to some royal family or other. It's a whopping great diamond and aquamarine affair set in white gold. There's extra security all over the place.'

'Is it very valuable?'

'My word, can you imagine the fuss if it went walkabout?'

Vanessa could. On one of her cruises, an American passenger had mislaid a ruby pendant. Everyone's cabin had been searched before the missing item of jewellery was found in a wastepaper basket. The passenger hadn't noticed it slide off the edge of her dressing table. The incident had unsettled everybody, and Vanessa could feel the same sense of unease tonight. If anything should go wrong, the crew would be the first to fall under suspicion.

'Is the ring insured?' she asked Kyle.

'The premium would be too high; it's priceless. That's why we're all running around like roos with our tails on fire.' Kyle grinned. 'Hey, did you and Lorenzo have a good day on the white sands beach? Word travels fast. He added, seeing the surprise on Vanessa's face, 'No need to answer. I can see you did. You've got the look.'

'What look?'

'Sort of sun-kissed.'

'It was nothing like that.'

'Course it wasn't,' Kyle hastened to agree with her. 'Well, make the most of it. Tonight's going to be a heavy one.' He stood to one side to greet an elderly gentleman. 'Can I help you, sir?'

'I'm lost,' he admitted, his face wrinkled with amusement. 'It happens all the time. May I join you?'

'We're about to have a staff meeting,' Kyle replied.

'I don't mind. You know I would prefer it. I don't like parties. People all talking at the top of their voices and saying nothing. But my daughter insisted I attend.' He beamed at Vanessa. 'Who do we have here?'

'This is Michelle Grant,' Kyle introduced her.

'How do you do.' The touch of his fingers was rough against Vanessa's as he kissed her hand. 'May I say that's a lovely dress you're wearing, a work of art. And you have beautiful blonde hair — a weakness of mine.'

'Thank you.'

Vanessa raised enquiring eyebrows at Kyle. The passenger was wearing a battered straw hat that looked incongruous with his evening dress, as did the well-worn trainers on his feet. His straggly grey beard could also have done with a trim. The brown eyes twinkled as if he was reading what was going through Vanessa's mind.

'You mustn't mind me, *cara*. I have a licence to do as I wish.'

'Mind if I leave you to deal with this one?' Kyle eased away.

'Do you know where you're supposed to be, sir?' Vanessa spoke carefully, not wanting to further confuse the elderly gentleman.

'I'm afraid I don't.'

'Do you know where your daughter is?' she persisted.

'She'll no doubt be about the place somewhere doing something important, I expect.'

'Shall we try and find her?'

'That's a good idea. Why don't we take a turn about the deck? Get some fresh air?'

'As you wish.'

'It's been a long time since a beautiful young woman has graced my arm,' he said wistfully. 'Tell me about yourself.'

Several of the guests who were gathered on the upper deck turned to look in their direction at the sound of their voices.

'You don't see your daughter anywhere, do you?' Vanessa was beginning to feel more uncomfortable by the moment.

'Do you think she's decorating the ballroom?' He chuckled. 'I peered through the doors. They've got balloons and streamers everywhere and a rotating glitterball. It painted exquisite patterns on the ceiling — a kaleidoscope of colours, as if someone had thrown a bouquet of flowers into the air. Would you like me to show you?' He tugged at Vanessa's arm.

'Papa, there you are. I've been looking for you everywhere.'

Vanessa almost sagged against the old man in relief.

'I told you we'd find her,' he chuckled happily. 'My daughter doesn't let me wander off on my own very often. I'm too much of a liability. Hello, darling. Michelle's been keeping me company. Do you two know each other?'

Vanessa didn't need to turn round. She had smelt that perfume on the launch this afternoon. It belonged to Claudia Amoretti, and she now realised the gentleman she had been escorting around the deck was the world-renowned artist, Claudia's father, the celebrated Severino.

'How many times have I told you not to wander off?' she chided her father in a gentle voice, a look of exasperation on her face.

'Many,' he said with a sigh. 'But I find it easier not to listen.'

'If you'll excuse me,' Vanessa began to make her apologies.

'No, I won't.' A stubborn look came into Severino's eyes. 'You must stay with me.'

'I don't believe we've met.' Claudia flicked a glance in Vanessa's direction.

'Then may I introduce Miss Grant to you,' Severino said.

'Michelle Grant?' There was no suggestion of warmth now in Claudia's voice.

'You know each other already?' Severino sounded disappointed.

'Mr Petucci mentioned the name to me,' his daughter replied.

Vanessa flushed, remembering their recent encounter on deck.

'I was hoping Michelle was going to be my friend for the evening,' her father said.

'Miss Grant is not a guest, Papa, and she has her duties to attend to.'

'Her duties are to look after these famous guests of yours, are they not?'

'Of course.'

'Then I want her to look after me.'

'I don't think that's a good idea.'

'Nonsense. You go off and have a good time with that young man of yours while Michelle and I get acquainted. Off you go now. Miss Grant — or can I call you Michelle? I would like a glass of champagne.'

Something in the tone of Severino's voice told Vanessa he was used to having his own way, and although he was charming, she wouldn't like to cross him. Neither, it seemed, did his daughter.

'If you're sure?'

'Absolutely. Come along, Michelle.'

'Mr Amoretti,' Vanessa protested, 'I really should attend my briefing.'

'The world knows me as Severino, my dear, and that is how you must address me.' He chuckled again. 'I'm a vain old man, but I do like giving orders. So where's that champagne?'

'I have to let Mr Talbot know where I am.'

'Claudia, you will give Miss Grant's apologies to Mr Talbot and tell him that she is otherwise engaged for the evening. There, now that's all sorted, I want to study the way the moonlight ripples on the water. Ah,' he accosted a passing waiter bearing a tray of drinks, 'thank you, young man. Can you tell me where we could get the best view of the moon tonight?'

Severino proved an entertaining companion as he regaled Vanessa with stories about his earlier days.

'Let us sit here,' he suggested after they had mounted the steps to the mezzanine deck. 'The breeze is strong tonight, also my legs do not support me as well as they did in the past.'

'Are you sure you're warm enough, Mr, I mean Severino?'

'With you beside me, I will never be cold.'

Although the elderly artist was flirting outrageously with her, Vanessa sensed his behaviour was more out of habit than anything else.

'You know,' he began, 'I love my daughter very much. She is so like her mother, my Maria.'

From the way he referred to his late wife, Vanessa sensed she had been the love of his life.

'I was years older than her. Her parents did not approve of me. I do not blame them. I was not a good choice of husband for their beloved daughter, an artist with no prospects and very little money. It was impossible.'

'Maria was your inspiration for *Il Pomeriggio*, wasn't she?' Vanessa remembered reading about it in her guidebook.

'Indeed she was. It was a beautiful afternoon and I was sitting in the sunshine. I had intended to have a snooze, but Maria began hanging out the washing. I watched her shaking out shirts and Claudia's little dresses, and that was when inspiration stuck. I had to capture that moment forever. Have you seen the painting?' Severino asked.

'Only copies of it.'

'Then after the party you must come to my studio. I will show you the original. Would you like that?'

'I'd be honoured,' Vanessa said.

'Good. Now I suppose I had better remember my manners and join my daughter and Mr Petucci.'

From the way Severino pronounced Giovanni's name, Vanessa guessed he would not have been the artist's first choice of husband for his beloved daughter. He leaned heavily on Vanessa's arm as she helped him up.

'I don't have so many late nights now,' he admitted. 'Thank you for your charming company. I look forward to seeing you again.'

After guiding Severino back to the ballroom, Vanessa hurried off in search of Lorenzo. She found him dressed in his white tie and tails, pacing the radio room.

'What happened to you?' he demanded. 'Kyle gave me some garbled story about you and one of the guests.'

'I got caught up with Severino on deck. He insisted I stay and talk to him.'

'Thank heavens you didn't bump into Claudia.'

'We did. Severino asked her to tell you where I was.'

'I didn't get the message.'

'I'm not surprised. She wasn't best pleased to be used as a messenger.'

Kyle poked his head round the door.

'You're on,' he announced.

'Right.' Lorenzo straightened his shoulders. 'Are we ready?'

With more guests having arrived throughout the afternoon, the ballroom was crowded; and with less room, Vanessa and Lorenzo were forced to perform a shorter version of the tango. Lorenzo seemed distracted, and they finished their dance to what was no more than polite applause. Everyone seemed to be having a case of the jitters, and Vanessa was glad this was her last night on board.

'Ladies and gentlemen,' Giovanni said as he strutted onto the stage just before midnight, 'I hate to interrupt the festivities, but I have an important announcement to make.'

A silence fell on the guests as they looked expectantly at the stage. Claudia, resplendent in her pale lemon evening dress, stood by Giovanni's side. Vanessa noticed that her smile did not reach her eyes. Severino was seated on a chair by the side of the stage. He caught Vanessa's eye and winked at her. Claudia followed his glance and looked as if she were trying to remember where she had seen Vanessa before. Vanessa shifted uncomfortably under the rotating glitterball.

Giovanni signalled towards the musicians. There was a drum roll, then another hush descended on the ballroom. Giovanni produced a small box and extracted a ring.

'It is with great pleasure that I can announce to everyone here that earlier this afternoon, Miss Claudia Amoretti consented to be my wife.'

He slipped the ring on her finger. As he bent forward to kiss her, Claudia moved her head fractionally away from his embrace. Giovanni was forced to kiss the edge of her ear. As he did so, a burst of applause broke out, and the band broke into a congratulatory song with everyone joining in. Then the lights were lowered, and Giovanni led Claudia onto the floor to perform their engagement waltz. Vanessa could not fault their choice of music or their perfectly executed dance steps, but it was a clinical performance, devoid of the starry-eyed emotion she would have expected from a newly engaged couple.

Severino, she noticed, had left his seat by the stage; and as other couples joined Claudia and Giovanni on the dance floor, she heard a voice say in her ear, 'Thank you for your company earlier this evening. And don't forget our date — to see *Il Pomeriggio*.'

Kyle held open the door and, thanking him, Severino departed the ballroom.

The party continued into the small hours. Vanessa's ankle began to throb, but she dared not leave the celebrations before Giovanni and Claudia departed. Eventually the waiters appeared with trays of fresh orange juice, and to her relief the party began to slow down.

'I suggest you make your exit now,' Lorenzo murmured in her ear. 'I'll cover for you.'

Vanessa nodded gratefully, made her

goodbyes, and hurried down to her cabin. Collapsing onto her bunk, she kicked off her sandals and massaged her sore feet. She was too stimulated to sleep. Was she the only one who had noticed something wasn't right between Giovanni and Claudia? Or had it all been a product of an overactive imagination?

Her mobile signalled an incoming text. Retrieving it from her bag, she switched it on. The message was from Michelle.

6

There was a gentle tap on her cabin door. Vanessa thrust her phone back into her bag. 'Who is it?' she called out.

'Lorenzo.'

She opened the door a fraction and peered out. 'Is something wrong?' she asked.

'Sorry to disturb you. Just checking you're OK.'

'I'm fine.'

He blinked, an uncertain look on his face. 'That's good.'

His answering smile was definitely on the nervous side. He looked uncomfortable standing in the corridor, but showed no inclination to leave.

'I can't ask you in,' Vanessa said, wondering what the true reason was for this midnight visit.

'No, that's not why I'm here.'

Vanessa raised an eyebrow. 'Isn't it?'

She was as perplexed as ever.

'Claudia didn't give you any trouble, did she?'

'No. Why should she?'

'That business with Giovanni. He is a bit of a ladies' man.'

Vanessa flushed again at the memory of their exchange on deck. 'I hope she didn't find out about it. I certainly had no intention of taking Giovanni up on his offer. Thanks again for rescuing me,' she mumbled, looking down at the floor.

'Don't mention it. What did you make of Severino?'

'Charming and roguish.'

'He has something of a reputation with the ladies as well. How did you bump into him?'

'I was on my way to the briefing. He was lost and looking for company. I didn't know who he was. Then Claudia arrived. She tried to take him away, but her father isn't a man to argue with.'

'I've heard he can be difficult.'

'He insisted I go up on deck with

him to look at the moon.'

'An original line if ever I heard one.' The corner of Lorenzo's mouth quirked into a smile.

'If there's nothing else,' Vanessa said in a slightly frosty voice, 'it's late.'

Lorenzo nodded. 'I've booked you on the ten o'clock launch back to the harbour tomorrow morning.'

'Thank you. I'll be ready.'

'What are you going to do now?'

'I'm going to try to get some sleep.'

Underneath his tan, he flushed. 'I meant when you get back to mainland Santa Agathe.'

'I'm not sure,' admitted Vanessa, reluctant to inform him that Michelle had been in touch and that they were due to meet up the next day.

'Do you have plans to fly back to England?'

'I may stay on for a few days; perhaps take in the sights.' Vanessa made a move to close the door, hoping Lorenzo would take the hint.

'They do trips up to the volcano, and

you can visit the hot springs or the amphitheatre. Then there are lots of interesting places down by the harbour. Santa Agathe is full of history.'

'Thank you. I'll bear your suggestions in mind.' Vanessa's arm was beginning to ache from struggling with the door.

The steward Lizabetta passed by in the corridor. 'Excuse me. Good night,' she trilled with the suggestion of a wink at Vanessa.

'I was wondering . . . ' Lorenzo lowered his voice. ' . . . maybe we could keep in touch?'

'I'm not sure,' Vanessa stalled, unable to come up with an excuse. Right now the thought of keeping in touch with Lorenzo Talbot was not high on her list of priorities.

'I would like to know what happened to your sister — for my records,' he finished lamely. 'In case there should be feedback.'

'You're not in any trouble, are you?' Vanessa felt a twinge of conscience.

Michelle was going to get the dressing-down of her life when they finally met up.

Lorenzo's tan deepened. 'It's an excuse, really,' he admitted. '*The Riviera* will be docked here for a few days, and I thought if you were still on the island, maybe we could do something together?'

Vanessa was glad the door was supporting her weight. 'I, um, can I let you know?' she asked.

Lorenzo's reply was a hasty, 'No pressure. Sleep on it.'

His departure was so swift Vanessa hardly had time to register he was gone. She stared after him with a mystified look, wishing she could shake off the suspicion that he had been detailed to keep tabs on her. Closing her cabin door, she reread Michelle's text suggesting they meet by the fountain in the main square. The message gave no clue as to where she was staying, what she had been doing or why she had asked Vanessa to take her place on *The*

Riviera. With a sigh, and too tired to think anymore, Vanessa turned out the light and went to sleep.

* * *

Claudia and Severino were waiting for the launch the next morning as Vanessa wheeled her suitcase along the deck.

'Good morning, Michelle.' Severino, still wearing his battered straw hat, kissed her on both cheeks. 'A night's rest has done you good. Your eyes, they sparkle, and I can smell the scent of lemons in your hair. You bring joy to an old man's heart.'

'Thank you,' Vanessa replied, wishing Severino did not have the power to make her blush.

She wondered whether or not it would be a breach of protocol to congratulate Claudia on her recent engagement. The facets of the diamond, almost too big for her finger, shone as they caught the early-morning sunshine.

'Are we to be travelling companions,' Severino asked, 'on the ten o'clock launch?'

'I believe we are,' Vanessa replied.

'Good. We can talk to each other while we are waiting. I want to learn all about you.'

Vanessa began to feel uncomfortable under his scrutiny. She didn't doubt Severino possessed a shrewd mind, and it wouldn't take much for him to work out she was hiding something.

'Papa,' Claudia interrupted, much to Vanessa's relief, 'don't detain Miss Blake. She has things to attend to.'

'Not now she doesn't. She's on her way home.' Severino assumed a look of mulish stubbornness. 'And aren't you forgetting something?'

'What?'

'You need to thank Michelle for looking after me last night.'

'It's really not necessary,' Vanessa came to Claudia's aid with a sympathetic smile.

'Actually,' Claudia surprised Vanessa

by saying, 'my father is right.' With an indulgent look at Severino, she said, 'When the mood is on him, he is a difficult man to defy. I should imagine he didn't give you much choice last night. Did he latch onto you?'

'I wouldn't go as far as to say that.'

'I would,' Claudia said with a wry twist to her lips.

'You make me sound like a scoundrel,' Severino protested.

'Which is exactly what you are.' Claudia linked her arm through the crook of her father's elbow. 'But don't ever change.'

Vanessa could barely contain her surprise. This was a side to Claudia she had not seen before. The affectionate teasing that went on between her and her father revealed a woman who loved Severino very much but was not blind to the older man's faults.

'Do you have children, Michelle?' Severino asked Vanessa.

'I'm not married,' Vanessa replied.

'Then may I offer you a word of

advice? Do not have a daughter. When they grow up, they boss you around and show you very little respect.'

'I'll bear your advice in mind,' Vanessa replied.

'Papa, the launch,' Claudia said sternly.

Still grumbling about ungrateful children, Severino allowed Claudia to guide him down the rope ladder. Vanessa looked over her shoulder. She had half-hoped Lorenzo would come to see her off, but there was no sign of him.

'Goodbye, Miss Blake,' Claudia said with a warm smile that completely transformed her previous unfriendly expression. 'I hope you have a safe journey home.'

The two girls shook hands; and Claudia, leaning over the handrail, waved them off as the skipper started up the motor. The sea was choppy, and Vanessa was forced to clutch the sides of the launch and concentrate on not feeling sick. She was glad the crossing to the mainland was only a short one.

'You must come and visit me at my studio,' Severino insisted as they disembarked. 'I will show you *Il Pomeriggio* and all my other work. It is an outstanding collection.'

Vanessa hid a smile. Severino displayed all the vanity of his calling.

'Ask anyone to show you the way. I'm quite famous, you know,' he added with childlike pride. 'Good day.' Tipping his straw hat to her, he ambled off in the direction of the town centre.

Vanessa glanced at her watch. Michelle had said she would be waiting for her by the fountain at eleven o'clock.

'The fountain is fifteenth-century, you know, and quite beautiful,' the skipper confided when Vanessa enquired the quickest way to the main square. 'You go up the hill then turn right by the memorial. You'll see a big plaque commemorating the safe deliverance of the community after a severe volcanic disruption. That's why the fountain was built, to teach future generations never to take the gods for granted.' Like all Santa Agathens, the skipper was proud of his heritage.

After thanking him, Vanessa set off up the hill, the heat of the morning sun bearing down on her back as she wheeled her suitcase over the cobbled stones. Away from the pressures of the yacht, she was able to think more clearly. Had Michelle been in Santa Agathe all the time? And if she had, why hadn't she honoured her booking on *The Riviera*? By the time Vanessa reached the memorial, she was out of breath, and her ankle was beginning to throb in protest.

'Nessa,' she heard Michelle calling out her name, 'over here.'

Vanessa squinted into the sunshine. Her sister was seated under a canopy outside an ice-cream parlour.

'I've ordered you one of these.' On the table in front of her were two huge sundae glasses filled with vanilla ice-cream and decorated with fruit, almonds and a raspberry topping. 'Local speciality, and the macaroons are to die for.' Michelle waved her spoon at Vanessa. 'I've already started mine. Tuck in.'

Vanessa pulled out a rickety chair and sank onto it, trying not to lose her balance. 'Hello, Michelle,' she greeted her sister in as calm a voice as she could manage.

'Oh dear.' Michelle made a face and dropped her spoon.

Although Vanessa was pleased to see her sister was safe and well, she was determined not to go soft on her. 'You're not pleased with me, are you?'

'You're right, I'm not.'

'What have I done now?'

'I hardly know where to start,' Vanessa admitted.

It would have been nice if Michelle had shown some remorse for all the trouble she had caused, but guilt wasn't her style.

'You'll feel less cross after you've eaten your ice-cream.' Michelle smiled.

'The peaches will sweeten you up.' She nudged the second spoon towards Vanessa. 'Try a mouthful,' she coaxed.

With a reluctant sigh, Vanessa dug her spoon into the soft almond-paste sundae.

'There.' Michelle was triumphant as a sigh of satisfaction escaped Vanessa's lips. 'I knew it would do the trick.' Her warm brown eyes sparkled with happiness. 'Now, not another word until you've finished every last scoop.'

In her haste to leave *The Riviera* and to avoid bumping into Giovanni Petucci, Vanessa had only drunk a cup of coffee for breakfast.

'I ordered these as well.' Michelle indicated a warm basket of freshly baked croissants. 'And some coffee. It's a good thing I'm here to look after you.' She spread cherry conserve over a croissant, broke it in half and handed it to Vanessa. 'Otherwise you'd starve.'

'There's no fear of that,' Vanessa said, savouring the aroma of the freshly brewed coffee.

'It is good to see you again.' Michelle's face was now lit up with happiness.

Vanessa's annoyance with her sister evaporated. Michelle could be the most infuriating of people, but she had a warm heart; and although the sisterly bond between them had been stretched to its limit on more than one occasion, it had never actually been broken.

'Do I get a kiss?' Michelle asked as Vanessa finished her cup of coffee.

To the indulgent smiles of their neighbours, Michelle didn't wait for Vanessa's answer. Instead, with a squeal of delight, she threw her arms around her sister's neck and hugged her.

'I've got such news for you,' she said in an excited voice.

'Such as where you've been this past week and what you've been doing?' Vanessa prompted.

'You'll never guess.'

'Enlighten me.'

'I've been getting married.'

7

'Isn't it exciting?' Michelle waved the third finger of her left hand under Vanessa's nose. She wore a shiny plain gold band. 'Say something,' she urged when her sister continued to gape at her.

'You're married?'

'I am,' replied Michelle, her smile growing wider. She clasped her hands together in a gesture of delight. 'He's the most wonderful man in the world. He was a passenger on my last Aegean cruise. He was on holiday on his own because a friend let him down.' Michelle hurried on with her explanation before Vanessa could intervene. 'I know what you're going to say about members of staff not fraternising with the passengers. But from the moment our eyes met across a crowded dance floor, it was as if no one else existed. He said I was the most beautiful woman he had ever seen, and we danced together all night.'

'You'll be telling me next you heard violins.' Vanessa knew she sounded grumpy, but right now she wasn't in the mood for a blow-by-blow account of Michelle's romance. She was in the mood for straight talking.

'I know it sounds corny, but that's how it was.'

'OK.' Vanessa knew from experience she was going to have to tread carefully if she was going to get any sense out of Michelle. 'So it was love at first sight?'

'Yes.'

'And when did you decide to get married?'

'When we realised we couldn't live without each other. We had to get married quickly, you see.'

Vanessa's concern deepened. 'Why?' she asked in a steady voice.

'Family problems.'

'You mean you're pregnant?'

'No such thing.'

'Then what?'

Michelle screwed up her face as if uncertain how to continue. 'His father wants him to marry the daughter of a family friend. The two fathers had sort of arranged it between them, for business reasons.'

'You're not serious? Things like that don't happen in modern-day Europe.'

'I know it sounds like something out of a movie, but that's how it was.' Vanessa could almost hear Michelle digging her toes in. 'Anyway, the daughter of this family friend didn't want the marriage either, and she had secretly got herself engaged to someone else. Isn't it thrilling?'

'That's not the word I would use,' Vanessa replied.

Michelle pouted. 'If you're going to be like this, I won't tell you the rest of my story.'

'Tell me about your wedding,' Vanessa coaxed in a softer voice, anxious to avoid a full-on sulk.

Michelle was all smiles again. 'Like I

said, we had to act quickly before the two fathers got wind of what everyone was up to. The arranged marriage is now totally out of the question, and there's nothing anyone can do about it.'

'And the wedding ceremony?' Vanessa prompted.

'I so wish you had been there, Nessa. We got married in a beautiful little church high up in the mountains, with only a cleaner and a gardener as witnesses. It was the happiest day of my life. We'll have a proper party later on when things are sorted out. You don't seem very pleased.' Michelle looked put out when Vanessa didn't respond.

'That's because I don't know what to say.'

'How about congratulations?'

'How about you explain exactly what is going on?'

'I don't understand.'

'I want the truth.'

'It is the truth.'

'And some,' Vanessa remained unconvinced.

'What's bugging you, Nessa?' Michelle was now red in the face. 'I thought you'd be pleased for me.'

'I'll tell you what's bugging me. I've been on board *The Riviera* for the past two days pretending to be you.'

'Why did you do that?'

'Because I thought I was helping you out. Or have you forgotten that tiny detail?'

'No, of course I haven't. But why did you pretend to be me?'

'Security reasons. There wasn't time to do a full check on my past. I've probably broken the law because of you.'

'Nothing went wrong, did it?' Michelle was now on the defensive.

'That's not the point. Giovanni Petucci thinks I'm you. What's he going to say when he realises that the person he thought was Michelle Blake was in fact her sister impersonating her?'

'He's not going to find out, is he? I mean, the gig's finished, isn't it?'

'It is. But if things should ever go

pear-shaped as a result of the subterfuge, I'm taking you down with me,'
Vanessa warned.

'You can't do that.' Michelle now
turned pale. 'Besides, I've done nothing
wrong.'

'You disappeared without a word,
leaving me out of my mind with
worry, and you call that nothing
wrong?'

'I suppose it was selfish of me.'
Michelle now sounded like the kid
sister in trouble, the one Vanessa had
dealt with so many times before.

'At last I seem to be getting through
to you.'

'I think you're being horrid. I'm in
love. You're jealous because I've found
someone to marry and you haven't.'

'Now you're being silly.'

'You are happy for me, aren't you?'
Michelle pleaded.

'Don't you realise it wasn't only me
whose life was disrupted?'

'No one else was involved, were
they?'

'Lorenzo Talbot put his job on the line.'

'Who is Lorenzo Talbot?'

Sensing intrigue, Michelle's eyes regained their sparkle.

'He's chief security officer on *The Riviera*.'

'Is he indeed? What's he like?'

'Your dancing partner was listed as Paolo Vargas.' Vanessa was determined to keep the conversation on track. 'He also failed to show. Do you have any idea what happened to him?'

Michelle squirmed in her seat. 'Yes.' She turned her head away, as if unwilling to look Vanessa in the eye.

'Well?' Vanessa waited. 'Are you going to tell me?'

Michelle looked back at her. 'He's my husband.'

'What?'

'Keep your voice down,' Michelle implored as Vanessa's heated reaction drew inquisitive glances from neighbouring tables. 'I am now Mrs Paolo Vargas.'

'What on earth are you playing at?'

'It seemed like a good idea at the time.'

'What did?'

'Getting the job on The Riviera. We cooked up the scheme between us because Paolo wanted to lie low for a while until we plucked up the courage to tell his father about us. As he can dance a bit, we thought we'd tell the agency arranging the gig that he was my dancing partner. They did all the registration stuff, I gave Paolo a few dancing lessons, and everything was fine. We were offered a contract.'

'What went wrong?'

Michelle raised her eyes in a gesture of exasperation. 'My passport expired. The cruise company used to take care of all that side of things, and we didn't realise until we got to the airport for the flight down here. It had expired the day before. We were frantic. I couldn't get a new one, as the old one was registered in my maiden name. It was a nightmare. We didn't want to lose the booking because we'd been paid an advance and already spent the money, so I came up with the idea of you taking my place.'

'You're going way too fast for me.' Vanessa put a hand to her aching head.

'Sorry,' Michelle apologised. 'I'm still on a high. Married life does that to you.'

'You and Paolo were stuck at the airport? Then what?'

'I've told you. I contacted you. I was so scared you wouldn't — '

'Why didn't you get a stand-in for Paolo?' Vanessa cut her short.

'There wasn't time. We were thinking on our feet.'

'Right.' Vanessa spoke carefully to slow things down. 'Where's Paolo now?' she asked.

'He thought he'd give us some time alone together. Wasn't that considerate of him?'

To Vanessa it sounded as though Paolo wanted to be out of the way when she starting asking awkward questions.

There were far too many gaps in Michelle's story for Vanessa's peace of mind.

'Does Paolo know you haven't got any money? If he married you for financial gain, he's out of luck.'

'That's an outrageous thing to say.'

'I'm being practical. How long have you known him?'

'Six weeks,' Michelle mumbled.

'Hardly a lifetime.'

'What is time? Anyway, what about you and that dreadful Charlie Hooper? You swore you were in love with him.'

'I was young. You're twenty-three and old enough to know better.'

'Nessa, let's not argue. I know you're going to adore Paolo. He's beautiful.'

'Beautiful or not, we could be in a heap of trouble.'

'What sort of trouble?'

'Fraud?'

'I think you've got a touch of the sun, Nessa. You need to chill out.'

'I need some straight answers.'

'I've given you them. There's no need

to be a crosspatch. I bet you were brilliant on *The Riviera*. And no one suspected anything, did they?'

'That's not the point.'

'From what you tell me, you sweet-talked that security guard Lorenzo into letting you on board. Now that I call style.'

'Will you stop talking nonsense?'

Michelle leaned forward and put her hand over Vanessa's.

'I got in touch with you as soon as I could, Nessa. Am I forgiven?'

Vanessa relented. She could never remain annoyed for long with Michelle. She was empty-headed, vain and self-centred, and never took life seriously; but she was also kind-hearted, and Vanessa didn't doubt that in her own way she was sorry.

'Michelle Blake, you are something else. How on earth did I allow myself to be talked into such a hare-brained scheme?'

'Sisterly love? And it's Michelle Vargas now.' Michelle was all smiles again. 'Let's talk about olive oil,' she suggested.

'I beg your pardon?'

'Olives? Those green things that grow on trees?'

'I know what olives are.'

'They can be purple too.'

'Get to the point.'

'Paolo's family grow olives. They run a huge farm. Paolo will be here shortly. He'll tell you all about it. He's so looking forward to meeting you. Immediately my new passport came through, he insisted we fly down here and explain everything. That shows you what a thoughtful person he is.'

The bell in the church tower chimed. Vanessa was surprised to see it was little more than an hour since she had left *The Riviera*. A shadow fell across the table.

Michelle looked up. 'Can I help you?'

'I very much hope so,' the man replied.

At the sound of his voice, Vanessa's

heart began to hammer inside her chest.

'Who are you?' Michelle demanded suspiciously, picking up on his unfriendly tone.

'This is Lorenzo Talbot,' Vanessa informed Michelle.

'The head of security?' Michelle cast a sideways glance of approval at Vanessa, then subjected Lorenzo to a brilliant smile. 'We meet at last. I'm Vanessa's sister, Michelle.'

'The one who went missing without a word?'

Lorenzo's voice was cold as ice. Michelle's smile faltered. 'I can explain about that.'

'I'm sure you can, but that's not the reason I'm here.' All the time he spoke, his eyes were fixed on Vanessa.

'I'm sorry I didn't contact you before I left *The Riviera*,' she apologised.

'Did you two have a date?' Michelle giggled, saving Vanessa from having to invent a valid excuse. 'Do you need a chaperone, Nessa?'

'I've come to inform Vanessa,' Lorenzo replied, 'that Claudia Amoretti's diamond and aquamarine ring is missing.'

8

Michelle's brown eyes lit up in disbelief as she turned on Vanessa. 'Claudia Amoretti was on board *The Riviera*? You didn't tell me, Nessa.'

'Concentrate, Michelle,' Vanessa snapped. 'Didn't you hear what Lorenzo said? Her ring is missing.'

'You didn't take it, did you?'

'The very question I was about to ask,' Lorenzo butted in.

'Of course I didn't. She was wearing it when I left *The Riviera*.'

'How do you know?'

'I saw it on her finger. She was arm in arm with Severino on the deck. He and I travelled back on the same launch. Ask him if you don't believe me.'

Michelle now leapt to Vanessa's defence. 'How dare you call my sister a thief?'

'I never said anything of the kind,' Lorenzo protested.

'Well I'm going to say something, so listen up.' Michelle tossed her head back in triumph. 'It's your fault the ring has gone missing, not ours. It happened on your watch. Nessa wasn't even on board. You heard her. The last time she saw this wretched ring, Claudia Amoretti was wearing it, and my sister doesn't tell lies.'

In that instant, Vanessa forgave her sister for everything. 'Thanks, baby sis.'

They slapped palms and grinned at each other.

'The Blake sisters rule,' Michelle trilled. 'Did you get all that, Mr Security Guard? We're innocent. Go find the guilty party someplace else. And . . . ' she added, getting into her stride, ' . . . in case you get any further ideas, Nessa hasn't slipped me the ring under the table to fence, or whatever it is you do when you steal something. You can search my handbag if you like.'

'I'm not accusing anyone,' Lorenzo

insisted in a quiet voice.

'Family honour is at stake here, so just to let you know, I'm onto your case.' Michelle sat back with a satisfied smirk and crossed her arms. 'Your call.' She waited for Lorenzo's response.

He looked puzzled, as if he wasn't sure what Michelle's outburst was all about. Privately Vanessa agreed with him, but she wasn't going to let on. Michelle had given them the upper hand, and she was determined to keep it.

'Have the police been contacted?' she asked.

'Giovanni wants to keep things low key. It may only have been mislaid. The guards are making a thorough search of the yacht right now.'

'Then shouldn't you be with them, directing things and identifying the real culprit?' Michelle demanded.

Lorenzo ignored her. 'It might be a good idea, Vanessa, if you don't leave the island.'

'You can't keep me here against my will.'

'Like it or not, you are a suspect.'

'How dare you?' Michelle was back on her high horse.

'Be quiet,' Lorenzo snapped, jolting her into temporary silence. 'I'll do my best to keep your name out of it, Vanessa, but you were on the yacht under false pretences.'

'Another fact you don't want coming to light,' Michelle intervened. 'It wouldn't look good, would it? Giovanni will go down the route that Vanessa couldn't have carried out the deception without your help. So you're in it up to your neck too, Mr Sunshine.'

'I don't need to remind you, Ms Blake that you were at the bottom of the reason for the deception.' Lorenzo's face was a mask of growing anger.

Although it was a warm day, it was all Vanessa could do not to shiver. There was no trace of the man who danced the tango with her now.

'Coffee, please,' Lorenzo accosted a

passing waiter, then drew out a chair and sat down.

The waiter was back a few moments later with a miniscule cup of dark liquid.

'When did Claudia notice the ring was missing?' Vanessa asked in an attempt to ease the tension from the situation.

'After you and Severino left.'

'Who is Severino?' Michelle asked.

'Claudia's father, and one of the most famous artists of his generation,' Lorenzo replied.

'I've never heard of him.'

Lorenzo picked up the menu and tapped on Severino's distinctive flowing signature displayed on the front. 'He lives on the island.'

Michelle studied the facsimile, a thoughtful look on her face. 'I think Paolo might have mentioned him.'

'Who is Paolo?' Lorenzo asked.

Vanessa felt an icy prickle inch up her spine.

'My husband,' Michelle admitted

proudly, displaying her new ring.

'You're married?'

'That's why Vanessa took my place. It was a whirlwind romance.'

'Did you know anything about this?' Lorenzo demanded.

'Don't start on my sister again,' Michelle insisted, 'she's innocent.'

'So you keep telling me.'

'Then why are you doubting my word?'

'I was under the impression the two of you had not been in contact with each other.'

'We haven't,' Michelle replied.

'Then why are you eating ice-creams together in the main square?'

'I can explain,' Vanessa insisted.

'I told Vanessa not to say anything,' Michelle said, raising her voice.

'Did you say your husband is called Paolo?'

'Yes.'

'Paolo Vargas?' Lorenzo asked slowly.

Vanessa didn't think it was possible for her heart to sink any further.

'That's right.'

'The same Paolo Vargas who is your dancing partner; who also went missing?'

'That's why neither of them turned up,' Vanessa explained. 'They were getting married.'

'And why I was forced to dance the tango with you,' Lorenzo added.

Michelle's eyes almost came out on stalks. 'You and Vanessa danced the tango?'

'Twice.' Lorenzo finished his coffee.

'Respect,' Michelle said, her voice filled with awe. 'Nessa, you are ace.'

Vanessa stared down at her empty sundae dish, her recently consumed ice-cream now making her feel sick. 'I am welcome?'

A scruffy-looking man dressed in ripped jeans and a crumpled T-shirt, with a growth of stubble on his chin, approached their table. Michelle leapt to her feet and threw her arms around his neck.

'Paolo, darling,' she embraced him.

'*Cara*, we've only been apart for an hour. Have a little dignity. What will your guests think?'

Lorenzo stood up. Paolo was tall, but Lorenzo was taller; and dressed in his casual security guard uniform of crisp shirt and tailored trousers, he provided a striking contrast to Paolo's urban chic.

'I am Lorenzo Talbot,' he introduced himself.

The two men shook hands.

'And you must be my new sister-in-law, Vanessa.' Paolo leaned forward and kissed her on both cheeks. 'You do not look like Michelle.' He frowned.

'Nessa always was the lucky one,' Michelle grumbled. 'I wish my hair was blonde.'

'Then I would not have married you,' was Paolo's brisk reply.

'Let's not go into all that now,' Vanessa was quick to intervene. Michelle was on high alert, and anything could spark off another heated interchange.

'You are right, Vanessa,' Paolo replied. 'Now is not the time for discussion; now is the time for celebration. You have heard, Lorenzo that Michelle and I have recently married?'

'Congratulations,' Lorenzo replied.

'Thank you. So, we will have some wine?'

'I have to get back to work.'

'You cannot stay?' Paolo looked disappointed. 'Vanessa, can you not persuade your friend to join us?'

'Lorenzo is not Vanessa's friend,' Michelle explained. 'He's chief security guard on *The Riviera*, Giovanni Petucci's yacht. Paolo, a valuable ring has gone missing, and Vanessa is the chief suspect.'

'This cannot be the truth,' Paolo responded. 'Lorenzo, how can you think such a thing?'

'I haven't accused anyone.'

'Yes you have,' Michelle insisted.

Vanessa decided to take charge of the conversation before Michelle said something they might all regret.

119

'Lorenzo, you are going to have to take my word for it that I do not have the ring, and that the first time I heard from Michelle was when she texted me last night just before you came to my cabin.'

'Hey, did I miss something?' A dimple dented Michelle's cheek. 'Smoochy dances? Midnight cabin visits? I always took you for a slow mover, Nessa, but this time I've been outclassed. You're not going to have to get married, are you?'

'Stop being childish, Michelle,' Vanessa snapped.

'You accused me of being pregnant,' Michelle retaliated.

Why was it, Vanessa thought in frustration, that every time she met up with her sister, it wasn't long before they behaved as if they were still at nursery school?

'Sisters.' Paolo raised his eyes at Lorenzo, 'I have three, all older than me, and when they meet up it's just like this. Do you have sisters, Lorenzo?'

'Two,' Lorenzo replied. 'That's why I can dance the tango,' he added.

A slow smile spread across Paolo's face. 'That I would have liked to see.'

'When you two have quite finished male bonding,' Michelle interrupted, 'I would like to go for a walk around the square. Someone mentioned a fiesta. There's going to be dancing and music.'

'It is an annual thing,' Paolo explained, 'to celebrate the summer. There will be a masked pageant later and a torch-lit procession.'

'I can't wait.'

'Unfortunately we cannot stay on,' Paolo said.

'Why not?' Michelle looked like a child denied a treat.

'I have been in touch with my father. My grandmother is not well. We have to fly home immediately. Vanessa, I am sorry,' he apologised, 'but you do understand?'

'When are you leaving?' Vanessa asked.

'As soon as I can make the arrangements.'

'But our celebration?' Michelle asked.

'It will have to wait. Vanessa, you will visit us as soon as possible?'

'She could come with us now,' Michelle suggested. 'That way I won't be on my own when you introduce me to all your scary sisters.'

'I am afraid not,' Paolo replied in a voice that brooked no argument.

'I can't leave her here on her own.' Michelle was putting up a spirited fight that Vanessa suspected was more to do with her nerves at meeting the Vargas family en masse rather than any sisterly concern for her welfare.

'I'll manage,' Vanessa insisted.

'Thank you, Vanessa,' Paolo said with a grateful nod. 'We will have one glass of wine, then I am sorry but we will have to leave you. Lorenzo, you will join us?'

'Thank you, but I really should be getting back.'

'Another time, then.'

Lorenzo looked at Vanessa. 'May I have a quick word in private?'

'I will order the wine,' Paolo said. 'Michelle, come with me.' With a firm yank of her arm, Paolo dragged her across the square towards a small trattoria opposite the fountain.

'I really think you ought to stay on here for a while,' Lorenzo insisted.

'How many times do I have to tell you I haven't got Claudia's wretched ring? You'll probably get back on board and find she left it in the bathroom or on a shelf or something.'

'Do you have to get back?'

'Not immediately,' Vanessa admitted, remembering her leaky houseboat was undergoing extensive repairs. 'Why do you ask?'

'It might be better if you stayed on until my enquiries are completed and you can clear your name.'

What Lorenzo said made sense. Vanessa didn't want the shadow of a jewel theft hanging over her head, and until the ring was found everyone was under suspicion.

'What are you going to do if you can't find it?'

'Let's hope you are right and it's merely been misplaced.'

'I suppose I could stay on for a few days and enjoy the fiesta,' Vanessa said. 'But where am I going to stay? I'm not going back on board *The Riviera*.'

'I'll see what I can arrange. Shall we meet back here this afternoon, three o'clock?'

'What about my luggage?' Vanessa looked down at her abandoned suitcase. The idea of trailing it around behind her all day did not appeal.

'You can leave it at any of the ice-cream parlours. It will be perfectly safe. I have to go. Until three o'clock?'

Vanessa watched Lorenzo stride off across the square, wondering if she had made the most foolish decision of her life. Was Lorenzo using her for his own means? It would be easy to blame the loss of a valuable ring on the most likely suspect, and masquerading under a false identity was as good a reason as any to nail Vanessa as that.

9

Brightly coloured flags flapped in the sunshine. Nearly every time she passed a display, stallholders accosted Vanessa insisting she taste some cheese or watermelon or a slice of almond pastry. Her polite refusals were met with beaming smiles, and although her knowledge of the local dialect was non-existent, vigorous sign language indicated that they thought she was too slender and needed feeding up.

Her blonde hair, too, was a source of attraction; and much to Vanessa's embarrassment, beaming suntanned matriarchs would drag various young men out from behind their stalls to admire it. Unused to such attention and having her hand kissed quite so often, Vanessa eventually sought refuge in a quieter corner of the square.

Ordering a fresh fruit juice, she

leaned back closed her eyes and allowed the heat of the day to play on her face until a dark shadow blotted out the sun.

'There you are.'

Startled, she opened her eyes. Severino was standing in front of her, his lined face creased in a happy smile. Raising his straw hat, he asked, 'Do you mind if I join you?' Without waiting for a reply, he sank down into the chair opposite with a heavy sigh. 'My legs are very unforgiving. They could do with a rest, as could I. What is that you are drinking?'

'Orange juice.'

'Then I will have some too.' He signalled for another glass, then settled himself more comfortably in his seat. 'You are staying on for the fiesta?'

'A few days, yes.'

'That is good. I will be your host.'

'I wouldn't want to be a nuisance.'

'Not at all. My daughter is always going off somewhere, so you can take her place.'

The waiter arriving at their table created a welcome diversion. Vanessa was not sure if Severino was up to date with all that had been happening on board *The Riviera*. If he didn't know about the disappearance of the ring, she was unsure if she ought to tell him.

Severino took the decision out of her hands by leaning forward and asking in a conspiratorial voice, 'What do you think of Giovanni Petucci?'

'I hardly know him.' Vanessa began to feel uncomfortable and hoped they weren't in for an in-depth discussion of Severino's future son-in-law.

'He is not the husband I would have chosen for my Claudia,' Severino admitted.

Unsure how to respond, Vanessa remained silent.

'She is so very dear to me, and all I have in the world, so you can understand my concern.'

'Naturally.'

'I suppose as long as she is happy, that is all I should worry about.'

'Where's your daughter now?' Vanessa decided it might be wise to pick on a neutral topic of conversation.

'She did tell me where she was going, but we mix in different professional and social circles. I stay at home. She travels the world.'

'I'm not sure I would want to leave Santa Agathe if it was my home.'

'My sentiments entirely. So tell me, what do you do when you are not sitting in cafés drinking fruit juice or dancing the tango?' The look on Severino's face turned into a gentle smile. 'What a charming blush. Have I said something to disconcert you?'

'I'm almost too embarrassed to say what I do for a living,' Vanessa admitted, 'now that I've given up professional dancing.'

'My dear, nothing you could say would ever shock me. Remember I am an artist. I have moved in bohemian circles all my life.'

'I paint portraits, makes sketches — little family pictures, that sort of thing,' Vanessa was forced to explain.

'That is wonderful. You must show me your work.'

'I couldn't.'

'Whyever not?'

'It's nothing compared to *Il Pomeriggio.*'

'Of course not,' Severino agreed, 'but how many people paint masterpieces, and who wants to buy them? The answer to both questions is hardly anyone. Whereas you, with your beautiful little portraits, have a ready-made market. And think of the joy they give to people.'

'You're very kind,' Vanessa said, touched by his praise.

'I am only speaking the truth.' Severino finished his juice. 'A picture painted with love is worth more than all the masterpieces in the world. You know, I have people praising my work, but they know nothing about art. They flatter me, but I can see through them. I may be old, but I am nobody's fool.'

Vanessa enjoyed talking to Severino.

He was a simple man with homely values.

'Those people on *The Riviera*,' Severino continued, shrugging his shoulders, 'they say clever things but they don't mean them. That is why I worry for my Claudia. I would not want her to forget her roots, and sometimes I think she is in danger of doing just that. But enough — we are here to enjoy the fiesta. Where are you staying?'

'Lorenzo Talbot is looking for a place for me. One of the crew rooms, perhaps,' Vanessa replied.

'Ah, your dancing partner. Tell him his services are no longer needed.'

'You're not offering to dance the tango with me in his place, are you?' Vanessa teased Severino.

'Much as I would love to, I fear my knees would let me down. What I actually meant was, you're staying with me.'

Vanessa decided it was time to take a firm hand with the elderly artist. 'No,

Severino. I couldn't do that.'

'Whyever not?'

She chose her words carefully, not wanting to upset him. 'It's not that I don't appreciate your offer . . . but no, thank you,' she added, unable to think of a valid reason to decline his invitation.

'You can occupy my villa as my special guest. I usually stay in the studio, and when I am working I do not emerge for days at a time.'

'Then having me there would distract you.'

'Not at all. I want to show you around. You can meet my friends. They will all be insanely jealous when they see how beautiful you are.' He chuckled. 'They might even think we are an item.'

'Severino,' Vanessa chided him, 'behave.'

'Sorry,' he said, looking anything but. 'If you are worried about the proprieties, there is no need. I have a housekeeper, Iolande Boniface — she will look after us both. There, it is all arranged. Now come along. I usually have a siesta about this time of day. You can escort me back to the villa, then you can tell your Lorenzo that everything is sorted. Not another word,' he insisted, sensing Vanessa's further protests.

'You must let me contribute something for my stay.'

'Having you there will be enough contribution. Now come along. Your arm, if you please.'

The walk up the hill was slow. Severino leaned heavily against Vanessa, and they made frequent stops while he caught his breath.

'I am sorry to be such a burden, Michelle.' He wiped his forehead with a spotted handkerchief.

'Actually, my name is Vanessa,' she admitted.

'That is the trouble with getting old, Vanessa. You get confused. I was sure your name was Michelle. I will try not to get it wrong again.'

'No, you didn't make a mistake,' she began to explain.

'It doesn't matter,' Severino insisted. 'I will call you Vanessa. That is all I need to know. We are nearly there.'

They stopped outside two huge barred gates. Through the railings, Vanessa could see a white-painted villa, its scarlet shutters closed against the fierce heat of the day.

'I have to have security,' Severino said as he pressed several buttons on an intercom system before there was a buzzing sound and the gates slowly opened, 'for insurance purposes. I do not like it, but what am I to do? It is an unfortunate reflection of modern life. Are we ready to go on?'

The pace of his steps was getting slower, and Vanessa was beginning to worry that his stamina would not hold out much longer.

A dark-haired woman bustled towards them. 'Maestro, what are you doing? You know the doctor has said you must rest. Who is this?'

'Jolly,' Severino greeted her with a kiss, 'this is my new friend, Vanessa. She is English, and she will be staying with us.'

The woman looked at Vanessa but did not smile.

'I'm sure it's not convenient.' Vanessa eased Severino's hold of her arm. 'I can find somewhere else to stay.'

'No,' the woman said as she shook her head. 'If The Maestro wants you to stay here, then you must.'

'Won't it make more work for you?'

'Yes, but that is my job. Now come along, Maestro. You are late for your siesta, and you know how bad-tempered you get when you are tired.'

Vanessa trailed behind them, feeling totally out of place. Olive trees shaded the path to the villa, and she welcomed the coolness on her skin after the heat of the climb up the hill.

'Please?' Iolande gestured towards a wooden door that had swung to after she had raced down the path to greet Severino. 'Would you open it? Thank you. Wait for me in the kitchen. It is at the back of the villa. I will escort the Maestro to the studio for his rest.'

Vanessa strolled out through the large doors that led from the kitchen onto the terrace, and caught her breath as she took in the view over the harbour. It was an artist's dream, and she could understand why Severino chose to live here. The sea sparkled like a jewel set in sunshine, and the neighbouring islands in the archipelago were tiny white dots in the distance. Vanessa turned as Iolande bustled back into the kitchen.

'All done. Now you would like something to eat?'

'No, thank you. I should be going.'

'Then we will have some coffee.'

Neither Iolande nor Severino seemed inclined to listen to Vanessa's objections to her staying at the villa.

'I have an appointment in the main square at three.'

'You can borrow the bicycle.'

'Iolande . . . ' Vanessa tried again.

'At the Villa Amoretti I am known as

136

Jolly,' she replied.

'Jolly, then. I know Severino was only being polite when he invited me to stay.'

'The Maestro does nothing out of politeness. I can assure you if he did not like you, he would not have invited you to stay.' Something resembling a smile crossed her careworn face. 'You are among a select number. I have worked here for ten years now, and in all that time I have known Severino to offer hospitality to no more than a handful of people. It is an honour,' she added with a significant look at Vanessa.

'Why me?' Vanessa asked, still totally perplexed.

'You are young.' Jolly's voice softened. 'The villa needs life. Miss Claudia does not stay often. The Maestro does not welcome her friends. They are too loud, too noisy. He likes beauty and peace. You must stay. And now you must hurry if you are to meet your young man in the square. The Maestro told me all about him as we walked down to the studio. He is a dancer too, like you?'

'No, he's in security.'

'If you would like to bring the gentleman up to the villa sometime,' Jolly continued, 'I will make you my special fish soup. No one makes the soup so good.'

Sensing she was being offered another honour, Vanessa meekly followed the housekeeper out of the kitchen, round the back of the paved terrace to where a tumbledown outhouse was hidden away behind more olive trees. She produced a bicycle of ancient origin

'It rattles, and you have to remember the brakes are not so good down the hill. Now off you go.'

To Vanessa's surprise, Jolly kissed her on both cheeks and stroked her head.

'Such lovely hair, like spun gold,' she said. 'The Maestro will enjoy painting you.'

'Painting me?'

'He is looking for a model for his

next masterpiece. It is to be called *La Sera* — *the evening*. He has made a wise choice.'

10

Lorenzo was waiting for Vanessa by the fountain as she wobbled to a halt. The bicycle made an agonising squeak of protest as she dismounted.

'Sorry I'm late,' she panted.

'Where did you get that?' Lorenzo stared at her dubious mode of transport. 'Out of a museum?'

'It's a long story.'

Vanessa pushed damp strands of hair off her face, wishing there was somewhere she could freshen up; but there hadn't been time at Severino's villa, and now she had other more pressing issues to face. How was she to tell Lorenzo of Severino's plans? She needed time to think straight, and to do that she also needed food. Lorenzo was standing in front of her, arms crossed, waiting patiently.

'Look,' she said, 'instead of talking

about museums, do you think we could get something to eat?'

'You're hungry?' Lorenzo drew reluctant eyes away from Severino's ancient bicycle.

'All I've had to eat today is an ice-cream with Michelle, and that was hours ago.'

'I know somewhere that serves pasta twenty-four seven, if you're interested.'

'I am,' Vanessa assured him.

She was glad Lorenzo knew where they were going as she followed him down a maze of winding back streets, past a medieval church smelling of incense and candles and a small market stall piled high with purple and cerise orchids.

An elderly lady hobbled towards Vanessa and expertly pinned a pink blossom in her hair. 'For you.'

'No, don't offer.' Lorenzo held Vanessa back as she attempted to pay for the flower. 'It would cause offence.'

'But aren't orchids expensive?' Vanessa asked in a low voice.

'Around here they grow uncultivated in the wild. Thank you, madam.' Lorenzo blew the stallholder a kiss and received a friendly wave in reply. 'Now if you want to get anything to eat today, come on.' He led her down more cobblestoned passageways.

'Is it much further?' She could feel a blister beginning to form on the back of her heel, and the strain of steering her bike and keeping to a straight path was making her arm muscles ache. Moments later, Lorenzo turned into a small square where a huge palm tree provided welcome shade. Several wooden benches and tables decorated with red and white checked cloths had been placed at convenient angles underneath it.

'Is this it?'

Lorenzo relieved Vanessa of her bike and leant it against one of the benches. 'Take a seat,' he invited.

'Where are we?' Vanessa looked round. Apart from themselves, the square was deserted. In the distance, she heard a cracked church bell chime the half hour.

'La Casa Di Manuela.'

'Manuela's House? They don't seem very busy.'

'That's because everyone is inside having a siesta.'

'If they're having a siesta, how on earth are we going to get served?'

'We sit down and wait.'

'For how long?'

'Embrace the culture.'

'What does that mean?' Vanessa was beginning to wonder if she had fallen off her bike and banged her head, when a fresh-faced waiter who looked no older than sixteen appeared by her side and delivered two steaming plates of pasta to their table. Convinced now she was imagining things, Vanessa leaned towards Lorenzo and whispered, 'We didn't order anything, did we?'

'That's the way things are done round here.'

The smell of wild fennel rising from

the steam made Vanessa's stomach rumble. 'What is this?' she asked, her mouth watering.

'It translates as sardine pasta. I presume you are still hungry?' He raised a questioning eyebrow.

The last of Vanessa's resistance collapsed. Following Lorenzo's example, she picked up her fork.

'Manuela will be mortally offended if you do not eat every mouthful.'

A jug of fresh water appeared on the table along with two glasses and a bowl of peaches. '*Buon appetito*,' their waiter said with a shy smile.

Vanessa stuck her fork into the soft creaminess of the macaroni, twirled it round, then swallowed a mouthful of delicately flavoured sardine that sent her tastebuds into overdrive. Lorenzo watched her with an amused expression on his face.

'I would suggest we don't speak for the next five minutes or so.'

With a mouth full of sardine, Vanessa could only nod her assent.

'That was the best meal I've ever eaten.' Vanessa finished the last of her macaroni pasta with a regretful sigh and delicately wiped her mouth with the huge paper napkin Manuela had provided.

'I'll tell Manuela the next time I see her.' Lorenzo offered the basket of peaches. 'You have to take one,' he insisted. 'It would be rude to refuse.'

'I feel like I'm a guest in someone's house,' Vanessa said, slicing into the ripe peach flesh.

'That's because you are.'

Juice squirted out of the peach as Vanessa's knife came into contact with the stone, leaving her face feeling sticky.

'Allow me.' Lorenzo leaned forward and wiped the moisture off her chin with the corner of his napkin. 'You are going to have to learn the art of quartering a ripe peach if you are going to survive in Santa Agathe.'

Vanessa did her best to concentrate

on what she was doing, but it wasn't easy with Lorenzo watching her every move. 'What did you say about us being house guests?'

'Manuela lives behind us.' Lorenzo indicated a sturdy stone building, its lemon-painted walls decorated with a fresco of orchids and olive trees. 'She opens her door every morning, then cooks a huge pasta that she tops up during the day. Guests are welcome to share her cooking and leave a contribution towards the costs on the table.'

'That's extremely trusting of her.'

'It's a trust that to my knowledge has never been broken. Now if you've finished battling with that peach, I suggest we make tracks back down to the harbour. I've got you a room.'

Vanessa wiped the last of the peach juice off her hands. 'That won't be necessary,' she replied, wondering if perhaps she should take up Lorenzo's offer of harbourside accommodation. She wasn't sure Severino's bicycle would survive the return journey up the hill laden with her suitcase, and the situation at the villa was highly irregular.

'You've not had a rethink about leaving the island, have you?' Lorenzo asked, instantly alert and no longer the lazy lunchtime companion.

Vanessa took a deep breath. 'Severino has offered me accommodation at the Villa Amoretti.'

After a short pause, Lorenzo asked with a frown, 'Are you sure? I mean, you didn't misunderstand him, did you?'

'I have a witness — his housekeeper Jolly; and she informs me that I've been accorded a rare honour.'

'You have indeed,' Lorenzo agreed. 'I've known journalists who would kill to get inside Severino's villa. You know he keeps *Il Pomeriggio* on private display in his studio?'

'He's offered to show me his collection.'

'Hm.' Lorenzo looked thoughtful.

'He's a difficult man to refuse,'

Vanessa said in an attempt to justify her decision.

'It's also going to be difficult to continue calling yourself Michelle.'

'I've already told Severino my real name is Vanessa.'

'How did he take the news?'

'He seemed to think it was his memory playing tricks on him.'

'Was it Severino who loaned you your transport?' Lorenzo's eyes now flickered towards the bicycle resting in the shade.

'That's why I was late,' admitted Vanessa. 'I don't think it's been used for years. Should I accept Severino's offer?' she asked, changing the subject.

'You have no choice. The Santa Agathens are fiercely proud. They do not make these gestures lightly. Today alone you have been offered orchids, sardine pasta and a room in Severino's villa. It is a mark of respect, so don't even think about rejecting Severino's offer.'

Vanessa put a hand to the orchid the

elderly stallholder had placed in her hair. The petals were velvet-soft and moist to the touch. 'Put like that, I can hardly refuse to stay at the villa, can I?' she said.

'That's what I want to hear.' Lorenzo smiled, actually looking pleased at the prospect.

'It's getting late. I should get back. It may take me two journeys to get everything up the hill.'

'I'll help you,' Lorenzo offered.

'Shouldn't you be back on board the yacht searching for the ring, unless you've already found it?'

Vanessa's flicker of hope died as Lorenzo admitted, 'It's still missing, and it's been a nightmare asking the guests if they would mind having their bags searched, but Giovanni insisted that no one was to be placed above suspicion.'

'Even me?' Vanessa knew she sounded churlish, but Lorenzo hadn't appeared to believe her when she told him Claudia had been wearing the ring when she had disembarked from *The Riviera*.

'I can't treat you any differently from the guests or the rest of the crew. You have to see that,' Lorenzo insisted. 'If it's any consolation, I am convinced you don't have the ring on you.'

'I could have passed it on to my sister.'

'You could have done. Where is she now?'

'Paolo is taking her back to meet his family.'

Lorenzo began counting out some change. 'That should do it,' he said, leaving the money on the table.

'Don't you think we ought to take it inside?'

'Manuela would be insulted if you did. Such an action would suggest the locals aren't trustworthy.'

'I don't think I'll ever get the hang of Santa Agathe,' Vanessa admitted.

'It takes years of practice,' Lorenzo agreed.

'How long did it take you?'

'I was born here,' he explained. 'My

mother was from the island.'

'You still live on Santa Agathe?'

'Not for many years. When my grandfather was alive, we visited every summer, but after he died we didn't come back so often. Then my mother fell ill.' A sad smile crossed Lorenzo's face. 'After she died, we lost touch with the island, but it's still in my blood.'

'And your father?'

'He was out here on holiday when he first saw my mother selling flowers in the market. He said it was love at first sight. After that, they rarely spent a day apart. They came from different cultures, but they were so happy together. I never heard them exchange a cross word.'

Vanessa looked down to where a butterfly had landed on the cobblestones. It flapped its scarlet wings as if testing them before flying off into the sunshine.

'Michelle said that's how it was with Paolo. Love at first sight.'

'And you didn't believe her?'

'Surely you have to know someone first before you can fall in love with them?'

'The Santa Agathen part of me would disagree with that statement. But that's not what's really worrying you, is it?'

'What do you mean?'

'I am half English, and the English side of me senses you are unhappy about something else besides the missing ring.'

Vanessa finished her glass of water to ease the dryness in her mouth. 'It's Severino,' she admitted.

'You feel uncomfortable about staying with him?'

'He wants to paint me.'

'You should be flattered.'

'He's planning a sequel to *Il Pomeriggio — the afternoon*. He's going to call it *La Sera — the evening*.'

'What a scoop. Don't tell anyone else. The media would go crazy.'

'I don't know anything about being an artist's model.'

'I'm sure it's nothing you can't handle. What is worrying you? Come on, out with it,' Lorenzo coaxed.

'Severino is used to having his own way.'

'Yes?'

'From what you said earlier, I can't really turn him down.'

'And?'

Vanessa knew she had turned an embarrassing shade of red. As if reading her mind, Lorenzo threw back his head and laughed out loud. Above them, someone opened a shutter and began to shake a rug out of the window. A dog began to bark. The square was waking up from its siesta.

'You're not scared Severino's going to ask you to pose for him . . . ' Lorenzo paused. 'How can I put it delicately? In a natural state?'

'It's not funny.' Vanessa was beginning to wish she had never raised the subject of posing for Severino. 'I'm used to portraiture — children posing for their grandmothers, couples, that

153

sort of thing. I told Severino about it, and I'm scared he might have got the wrong idea about my artistic background.'

'I'm sorry.' Lorenzo wiped his eyes with the back of his hand. 'I shouldn't have laughed.'

'No, you shouldn't.'

'You want my advice?'

Vanessa nodded.

'Go for it and you needn't worry about a thing. You have my word as a native of Santa Agathe.' Lorenzo leaned across the table and squeezed her fingers. 'What makes Severino's work so individual is his style. Ordinary people leading ordinary lives, that's what he does best. He's probably imaging the evening sun spinning gold into your hair and you sitting on a stool preparing vegetables for the evening meal, and you can't get much more ordinary than that.'

Lorenzo's words should have eased Vanessa's fears, but they didn't. She knew that far from being an island of magic, Santa Agathe was an island of surprises, the latest one being how she was beginning to feel about Lorenzo Talbot.

11

'Such terrible news.' An agitated Jolly was peering through the railings as Vanessa and Lorenzo approached the Villa Amoretti. Her wrinkled face was screwed up in anguish, and she was clutching a damp tissue as with trembling fingers she keyed in the security code to activate the gates. They slowly parted to let Vanessa and Lorenzo through.

Jolly cast an anxious look over their shoulders. 'Quickly, hurry. They may still be lurking in the bushes.'

Vanessa wheeled her bicycle onto the grass. 'Jolly, calm down and tell me what's upset you.'

Jolly barred Lorenzo's path as he tried to follow Vanessa. 'Who are you?'

'My name is Lorenzo Talbot.'

Vanessa moved in front of him, scared Jolly was going to attack him.

'Lorenzo was born on Santa Agathe,' she said.

'But he is English like you.'

'I'm Gina's son,' Lorenzo said, wrapping his hands around Jolly's trembling fingers.

'Gina Albani?' she queried in a trembling voice.

'That's right.'

'Your mother used to sell flowers in the market?'

'With her father, my grandfather. He was also called Lorenzo.'

'I remember.' The anguish left Jolly's face. She eyed the blue and white logo on Lorenzo's shirt.

'Lorenzo has been working with me on *The Riviera*, Mr Petucci's yacht,' Vanessa explained.

'Can I come in?' Lorenzo dropped his hold on Jolly's hand and stood deferentially to one side of the iron gates.

'The Maestro does not like uninvited visitors.'

'But he knows Lorenzo,' Vanessa

insisted. 'They were together on *The Riviera*.'

'What am I going to do?' Jolly pleaded with the pair of them.

'What's happened?' Vanessa spoke slowly, not wishing to further agitate her.

'I was preparing your room, Vanessa, so I wasn't with the Maestro. I blame myself.' She wrung her hands in a gesture of distress. 'The doctor has only just left. You did not pass him?'

Vanessa glanced towards Lorenzo. She was now beginning to feel seriously concerned. 'We saw no one.'

'Maybe he has been attacked, too.'

'Severino's been attacked?' Vanessa could feel her own panic rising.

'Why don't we walk down to the villa and make ourselves comfortable — then you can tell us what this is all about?' Lorenzo took charge, gently guiding the trembling Jolly away from the open gates. He pressed the security button and they swung back into place. 'There now,' he reassured her, 'we are safe, and I am sure nothing has happened to the good doctor, so don't concern yourself on his account.'

'You're very kind.'

Jolly began to regain her composure, and the little group trundled down the hill, while she dabbed every so often at her face with the corner of her sleeve, her damp tissue now in shreds.

'You can leave the bicycle by the entrance to the basement, and the luggage in the vestibule there,' she instructed them. 'It's this way.' She led them through the darkened parlour and out onto the terrace. Coloured bulbs strung across the bougainvillea cast little pools of light on the flagstones. Jolly drew out some chairs. Murmuring their thanks, Vanessa and Lorenzo sat down.

'Tell us exactly what happened,' Lorenzo encouraged Jolly.

'You would like something to drink first perhaps?' In her agitation, Jolly seemed unable to sit still for more than a few moments. She looked to Lorenzo for authority, and Vanessa allowed him to take charge of the situation.

'Later,' he replied in a gentle voice. 'Now what has upset you so badly?'

Jolly took a deep breath. 'There was a break-in.'

'Severino wasn't harmed?' Vanessa felt sick in the pit of her stomach at the thought of anything happening to him.

'No. He was asleep. He said the noise woke him up. I saw his light on and I raced down to the studio. The Maestro was so upset that I called the doctor and he prescribed a sedative.'

'What did Severino see?' Lorenzo asked.

'A young man running off with one of his paintings.'

'Why didn't the alarm sound?'

'The Maestro hates security. He says the flashing light keeps him awake even though he can't see it, but sometimes he turns it off. I am to blame. I should have checked. I usually do; but with your arrival, Vanessa, I had other things on my mind.'

'What happened wasn't your fault, Jolly.' Vanessa stroked her arm. The gesture seemed to comfort her. She squeezed Vanessa's fingers with her other hand.

'I should have run after the culprit.'

'I'm very glad you didn't.'

'If I had caught him, I would have broken his legs,' Jolly insisted.

'No you wouldn't,' Vanessa contradicted her. 'Where would Severino be if you were charged with assault?'

'He would stand by my side.'

'You must leave that sort of thing to the authorities.'

'Pah, what do they know?' Jolly was beginning to regain her composure. 'They are nothing more than a bunch of young boys.'

Vanessa cast Lorenzo a look of desperation.

'Vanessa's right, Jolly. You can't go taking on intruders. You might get hurt.'

A sulky look crept across her face.

'I want your promise,' Lorenzo insisted.

'Who are you to make me promise

such things in my own home?'

'Someone who knows how dangerous intruders can be. Do we have your word you won't do anything silly?'

Lorenzo waited patiently for Jolly to agree with him. She nodded reluctantly. 'I promise,' she said.

'Good. Do you want me to have a look round and check up on things?' he asked.

'Nothing is missing except *The Harbour at Sunset*. It is one of the Maestro's favourites.' Jolly's voice began to shake with emotion. 'He will be so upset when he wakes up.'

'I'll make sure the doors and windows are secure,' Lorenzo offered.

Jolly's bravado seemed to be wearing off. 'You won't wake the Maestro?'

'I'll be as quiet as a mouse. You stay here.'

They watched Lorenzo head down the path towards the studio. Dark shadows created eerie silhouettes as he skirted the flower borders, dislodging blossoms in his wake. Vanessa's eyelids began to droop. It had been a long day, and it wasn't over yet.

'I don't think the Maestro would mind if Lorenzo wished to stay on for the night,' Jolly suggested in a gesture of reconciliation. 'I'm sorry if I was rude to him earlier. You will explain and apologise for me?'

'Lorenzo will understand,' Vanessa assured her. 'But he can't stay. He has to return to Mr Petucci's yacht. There's no need to worry. I'll be here, and as long as we make sure the alarms are reset, everything will be fine.'

'I was silly not to believe the rumours.'

'Rumours?' Vanessa questioned.

'There have been stories of a gang coming over from the mainland, breaking into properties and stealing valuables to order. There is a thriving business in art robbery. Jewellery too,' Jolly added.

Her words made Vanessa shiver. 'Where did you hear these rumours?' she asked.

'It is common knowledge in the square. A lot of people like Mr Petucci are attracted to the islands. They come here to relax because they are made welcome. They bring much-needed income to the area. They buy property and they spend their money. Some of the villas are exquisitely furnished, although I have never been inside them.'

'Have there been other incidents?' Vanessa asked.

'Only stories, I think. I will ask my friends tomorrow.'

The sound of footsteps in the darkness drew their attention back to the path leading down to the studio.

'Nothing to report,' Lorenzo informed them. 'I looked in on Severino. He is fast asleep, and the windows and doors are secure.'

'To think such a thing could happen on Santa Agathe. We have always trusted each other, but now that trust has been broken. Things will never be the same again.'

Vanessa did her best to raise Jolly's dampened spirits. 'Yes they will. One incident like this doesn't make Santa Agathe a major crime scene.'

'You think I am being silly?'

'Not at all. You've been extremely brave.'

'I am nothing but a foolish old woman.' Jolly struggled to her feet.

'You're anything but, Jolly,' Vanessa insisted.

'No more talk of gangs and jewel thieves. You are here on holiday, and as a native Santa Agathen, it is up to me to see that you have a good time.'

Vanessa smiled, but deep down she couldn't shake off her worries. Had *The Riviera* also been targeted, with Claudia's ring disappearing at the same time as Severino's *The Harbour at Sunset?*

'We mustn't forget the summer fiesta, either. The Maestro has promised to honour several events with his presence. That will take his mind off art robberies,' Jolly said.

'Have you called the police?' Lorenzo asked.

'The Maestro does not want them here. He will tell us what he wants to do in the morning.'

Lorenzo glanced at his watch. Jolly picked up on the gesture. 'We are keeping you?'

'I should get back to the yacht.' He looked at Vanessa. 'Call me day or night if you are worried about anything.'

'Why don't you walk Lorenzo back down to the gates, Vanessa, while I prepare us a light supper? I have some ham with salad and fruit and biscuits.' She bustled off towards the kitchen.

Lorenzo and Vanessa strolled down the drive as the night sky turned a deep purple. 'You're happy to stay on at the villa?' Lorenzo asked.

'I can't leave now, can I?' admitted Vanessa. 'But supposing whoever it was come back? I don't think the three of us would be much of a match for a determined gang of art thieves.'

'I have a local contact in the police.

I'll ask him to keep a discreet watch on the place.'

'They could be after *Il Pomeriggio*.'

'Hardly. It's too famous.'

'If it was passed on as a copy, people would still pay good money for it, wouldn't they?'

'You're entering the realms of fantasy,' Lorenzo chided. 'Steady,' he said as he caught Vanessa's arm after she lost her footing.

The heady fragrance of frangipani was beginning to sway her senses from crime to an emotion of a more intimate nature. In the distance she could hear the soothing sound of the sea against the vibrant chirp of cicadas.

'You're shivering.' Lorenzo secured his arms around her waist. 'Are you cold?'

'No,' Vanessa replied, wishing he would loosen his hold. It was so difficult to resist the temptation to rest her head on his shoulder. She wanted nothing more than to fall asleep exactly where she stood.

'Promise me one thing,' Lorenzo said, his lips moving closer to her ear.

Vanessa could feel her willpower ebbing out of her control. 'What?'

'You won't do anything silly.'

Vanessa jerked back to reality, determined not to let the romance of the night dismantle her self-control. 'Such as?'

'Tackling intruders?'

'You said they wouldn't come back.'

'In case they do.'

'Nothing happened until I turned up on the island, did it? Now rings are missing and paintings are being stolen. You think I'm responsible, don't you?'

Vanessa knew she was being irrational, but she was too tired to think straight. She wanted Lorenzo to get angry with her and just go. 'That's what you really think, isn't it?' She turned her face up to his, too late realising what was going to happen but lacking the willpower to stop it.

'I'll show you what I have been thinking of doing for the last half hour.'

As his lips touched Vanessa's, they melted away the worries of the day. She wasn't sure how many moments passed before Lorenzo released his hold.

'There, now you know what I really think. I was wondering what it would be like to kiss you. Try to get a good night's sleep.'

The iron security gates opened slowly and Lorenzo passed through them. Vanessa waited where she was until the sound of his footsteps disappeared into the night. She suspected a good night's sleep was the last thing she would get.

12

Feeling more than a little self-conscious, Vanessa set up her easel in the market square. This sort of thing wasn't her style, but Severino was adamant and had addressed Vanessa in the tone of voice she was beginning to recognise. He meant to have his way.

'I am tired. Today I do not paint. The fiesta will have to function without me. You will go as my representative.'

'Wouldn't it be better if I stayed here with you at the villa?' Vanessa said, attempting to stand her ground. 'I could help Jolly.'

'People will not understand why there is no Severino presence at the festival. Go and explain. Do not say I am tired; say I am on a creative surge,' he instructed with a twinkle in his mischievous eyes.

'Do as the Maestro says,' Jolly

advised when she caught the tail end of the discussion. Then she sent a guarded look in Severino's direction and whispered in Vanessa's ear, 'But no talk of break-ins.'

Severino, with his eyes now closed, appeared not to hear the hushed exchange.

'Rumours circulate like mountain fire around the island,' Jolly added, 'and we do not want gossip getting out of control.' She hustled Vanessa out of the studio.

'What excuse can I use for being there?' Vanessa protested. 'People won't recognise me.'

'They will know you are Severino's guest, and they will treat you with respect.'

'How will they know I'm staying here?'

'Don't ask so many questions. Here, you can take these.' Jolly thrust an easel and painting materials into Vanessa's hands. 'Now off you go and paint your little pictures.'

'I can't paint a portrait without preparation.'

'Then follow the example of the great masters. Sketch.' Jolly made a gesture with her hands that suggested Vanessa was making a fuss about nothing. The doctor's arrival interrupted what was promising to turn into another animated exchange.

'I will give you a ride down to the harbour,' he offered, 'after I have had a word with the Maestro. I won't be long.'

'There. No more fuss. You go.' Jolly crossed her arms, a triumphant look in her eyes.

'What if there's another attempted break-in while I'm out?'

'I will break their legs.'

'Jolly, I'm serious.'

'So am I. I will make sure the Maestro does not disconnect the alarm, and a nice policeman called by this morning before you were up. He said he was acting under instructions from Mr Talbot, and he promised to keep an eye on us.' A sly look crossed Jolly's face. 'Your Lorenzo is a good man. Under his protection we will be safe.'

Mention of Lorenzo's name made Vanessa blush.

'I knew it,' Jolly crowed. 'You are lovers.'

'Jolly, please.' Vanessa pretended to check her painting materials.

'Please what? There's no need to blush like a schoolgirl. He is handsome. You are beautiful. It is perfect.'

'It's not.'

'Not what?'

'Anything.'

'I looked out the window last night. When the security light came on, I saw him kiss you. It was very passionate.'

'There's the doctor,' Vanessa said in relief as he joined them on the terrace. She didn't want to think about Lorenzo's kiss. Jolly's revelation that she had been secretly looking on could only make things worse. She was sure the housekeeper wasn't a gossip, but could she keep quiet about what she perceived as a romance?

Vanessa still couldn't understand what had motivated Lorenzo to do such a thing. Much to her annoyance, her lips still tingled at the memory.

'I have insisted that the Maestro rest,' the doctor informed them. 'There could be a delayed reaction. He is not a young man.'

'Should I contact his daughter?' Jolly asked in concern.

'I don't think that will be necessary, but I am glad you have Miss Blake here with you to keep an eye on him. The Maestro has a habit of not doing as he is told.'

'The Maestro is his own man,' Jolly said with a trace of pride.

'I don't doubt that; but you must insist he doesn't overdo things, otherwise I will not be responsible for the consequences.'

'And the fiesta? There will be many disappointed people if he does not attend any of the events.'

'I will call again tomorrow and we

174

can see how he is, but for the moment he does not leave the villa. Now, Miss Blake, are you ready?'

'It's Vanessa,' she insisted.

'Very well, Vanessa. I understand you are an artist too?'

'I only dabble.'

'That's is good,' the doctor replied with a friendly smile. 'There are enough temperamental artists on the island who all think they are the next Severino. Still,' he added as he snapped his bag shut, 'I shouldn't complain. Their nerves keep me in business.'

'Come along,' Jolly said as she bustled about, picking up Vanessa's belongings. 'The doctor is a busy man. Don't keep him waiting.'

★ ★ ★

Down in the square, Vanessa was now the centre of curious looks from passersby. Word had got round that she was here on behalf of Severino, who had been unavoidably detained. She smiled at a group of children, who giggled and ran away. One of the bolder boys dared to edge forward. With the help of sign language, Vanessa managed to convey that she would like to make a sketch of him.

The man behind the fish stall had been watching their pantomime with a show of interest. 'I translate,' he said. 'My name is Mauricio. I sell the best fish on the island.' They shook hands. 'I will now tell my grandson to sit still and not fidget.'

He produced a wooden seat, and with a little encouragement the child perched on it, a cheeky smile on his face. Soon a large crowd had gathered around them. Vanessa lost her feeling of nervousness as she began to outline the child's face. He proved an interesting subject, and under his grandfather's watchful eye sat very still. As Vanessa finished her pencil sketch, the spectators broke into a round of applause.

'They like,' Mauricio said. 'You will do another? Hey!' He caught his grandson by the scruff of his neck as he made to run away. There followed a rapid exchange that Vanessa could not follow. 'We have a box,' Mauricio explained, 'for charity. My grandson will take charge of donations. If people want you to draw their portrait, they pay.' He rubbed the tips of his fingers together, gesturing payment. 'OK?'

Vanessa was kept busy all morning, and soon the wooden box was heavy with donations. Mauricio appointed himself as Vanessa's minder, and kept her topped up with refreshing drinks. Later in the morning he purchased two cones from the makeshift gelateria set up under a jaunty red and white sunshade.

'We take a break,' he said, and lowered his vast weight onto the vacated chair opposite Vanessa. 'You like?' he asked, indicating the creamy confection. 'It is a speciality of the island, vanilla flavoured with almonds and honey.'

Vanessa nodded as the soft gelato

eased the dryness in her throat. Mauricio gave an approving nod.

'You stay with the Maestro?' he asked, applying himself to his own gelato.

'Yes,' Vanessa replied, wondering yet again how far the word had spread.

'We look after him,' Mauricio explained. 'He is a son of the island. It is good that he has a beautiful lady to stay at his villa.'

Vanessa wished the Santa Agathens would stop referring to her as beautiful. At school she had always been on the lanky side, and her blonde hair had been nothing special. The Mediterranean sunshine had lightened it a shade or two, and that was what she supposed made her different. The local women were mostly dark-haired.

'Would you like me to draw you?' Vanessa licked her fingers as she finished her gelato.

Mauricio did his best to protest, but he wasn't very convincing; and like his grandson, he proved an interesting

178

subject. He picked up his finished portrait with a huge smile that almost split his face in two.

'The Maestro he has competition, no?' He laughed and showed the sketch to his fellow stallholders.

'Excuse me.'

Vanessa turned. A man was standing to one side, clutching a child's hand. 'Can I help you?' she asked.

'You are about to have a siesta?'

It was then Vanessa noticed that the stallholders were beginning to close up. 'I wasn't, but business appears to be slowing down.'

'Would you have lunch with me and my daughter?'

'I don't think — ' Vanessa began.

'It is not good for you to sit out in the heat of the day. Your pink hat will not afford much protection, and you need to protect your shoulders.' He indicated Vanessa's sundress. 'And,' he added, 'you need to eat.'

There was something about the way he spoke that reminded Vanessa of someone; but before she could reply, the little girl tugged at her father's hand and whispered in his ear. The man straightened up when she had finished and said, 'Assunta thinks you are very pretty, and she would like you to join us. You can leave your things here. No one will touch them.' He began to stack her easel against Mauricio's stall. 'My name is Carlo Boniface.' He looked expectantly at Vanessa.

'I'm sorry?' she said with an embarrassed smile. 'Should I have heard of you?'

'You do not recognise me?'

Vanessa was forced to shake her head.

'No matter,' Carlo brushed aside her discomfort. 'Unlike Severino, I am not famous. Come, I know a very nice trattoria. It is one of Assunta's favourites and it isn't far.'

Much to the disappointment of her patron, Vanessa opted for a light salad. 'You are on a diet?' Carlo asked, ordering the more substantial fish platter for himself and a child's portion for Assunta.

'Mauricio treated me to gelato,' she explained. 'I'm not that hungry.'

'Santa Agathe has the best gelato in the world,' he announced.

Vanessa, who was getting used to local pride in their small island, smiled in agreement.

'Do you enjoy staying at the Villa Amoretti? I heard you talking to Mauricio,' Carlo explained.

'Very much.' Vanessa decided to gloss over recent events.

'Are you on holiday?'

She hesitated, uncertain how to reply to the question, then decided to stick to the truth as much as possible. 'I was working on Giovanni Petucci's yacht, *The Riviera*. When my contract finished, I decided to stay on here for a few days.'

'You have picked a nice place,' Carlo agreed. 'The view from the villa is especially beautiful this time of year.'

'Have you been there?'

'You sound surprised.'

'From what I've been told, Severino doesn't encourage visitors.'

'I know he lives in the studio, and that is where he keeps *Il Pomeriggio* and his other works of art; and I also know he is very lax about security.'

Carlo's charming smile did nothing to ease Vanessa's suspicions. Was she being sounded out as a possible link to Severino? And if so, why? She tried to remember what Jolly had said about art thieves targeting the island. Petty crooks were sometimes the last people you would suspect to be guilty of such a crime. And if that was the case, Carlo fitted the bill.

Assunta again began to whisper excitedly in her father's ear before Carlo chided her, 'It is rude to whisper in front of our guest.' He smiled across at Vanessa. 'It is her grandmother's birthday next week, and we think a portrait would make a nice present.'

Vanessa relaxed. 'Is that the reason for the lunch?'

'Partly,' Carlo admitted. 'And of course it will do my street cred no harm to be seen lunching with the remarkable Miss Blake.'

'Remarkable?'

'You're different,' Carlo confided, 'and the Santa Agathens love a romance. I heard something about you and Gina Albani's son?'

'There isn't a romance.' Vanessa was growing weary of emphasising her single status.

'Then they will invent one. You must not be annoyed. The Santa Agathens would not do it if they didn't like you.'

'I suppose there are worse things that could happen,' Vanessa agreed.

'That's it,' Carlo approved. 'Best not make a fuss. Let the gossip die down.'

'To get back to business, I can make a start on your daughter's portrait after lunch,' Vanessa said, turning the conversation away from gossip and romance.

'Excellent. You hear that, Assunta? Say thank you.'

The child, overcome with an attack

of shyness, murmured a reply.

Vanessa's salad arrived at the table, and although her appetite had now completely deserted her, she made some pretence of eating. 'Do you live on the island?' she asked Carlo.

'I have a home here, but I work in technology and it can take me all over the world. When I am away, my mother looks after my daughter.'

'And your wife?'

'I am single,' Carlo replied, his body language discouraging further questions. He signalled for the bill.

'Please, let me contribute.'

'No, I invited you,' he said when Vanessa began to search for her purse. 'Perhaps you would keep an eye on Assunta for a few moments while I settle up?'

The child blew contented bubbles down the straw of her drink, giving Vanessa the chance to look round the busy trattoria. Every table was occupied, and although she did not recognise anyone, several people smiled in her direction. Anxious to discourage further speculation regarding her personal life, she returned their smiles, then glanced determinedly out of the window.

Carlo appeared to be engaged in a discussion with another man. Vanessa bit down a cry of surprise as he moved to one side, revealing the identity of his companion. The man he was talking to was her new brother-in-law, Paolo Vargas.

13

'I'm sure there's a logical explanation.'

Lorenzo and Vanessa sat on the harbour wall, a light breeze whipping up white crests on the water below as it lapped the shoreline.

'I've thought of every possible reason why Carlo should have been talking to Paulo, and none of them are logical,' Vanessa insisted. 'Paolo and Michelle were supposed to have flown off the island to visit his sick grandmother. Michelle even sent me a message to say their flight had been called.'

'It couldn't be a simple case of mistaken identity?' Lorenzo asked.

'No way. It was Paolo Vargas. I'm certain of that.'

'Why didn't you speak to him?'

'I don't know. I sort of froze. I had Assunta with me, Carlo's daughter, and I couldn't rush out and leave her.'

'And Michelle wasn't with Paulo?'

'No.'

'Have you heard from her again?'

'She only ever seems to get in touch when it suits her.' Vanessa's patience was being stretched to the limit. 'What can she be up to?'

'Have you tried asking Carlo why he was talking to Paolo?'

'We're hardly on those terms. Besides, it would sound as though I'm spying on him. I only met him this morning — and that's another thing.' Vanessa clutched Lorenzo's arm. His flesh was warm to the touch, but she hardly noticed. 'Carlo knows all about the Villa Amoretti.'

'A lot of people do. It is a local landmark.'

'Not everyone can list Severino's paintings in detail or describe the view from the terrace. He's been there, I'm convinced of it — and you know Severino discourage visitors.'

'You're making it sound as though this Carlo has been casing the joint,'

Lorenzo said with the suggestion of a smile.

'Don't you think his behaviour is odd?'

'Are you sure you're not overreacting?' Lorenzo sounded infuriatingly unperturbed. 'You've had a lot on your mind recently.'

'My judgement's not clouded and I am not imagining things.'

'Have it your own way. But if you want my opinion, I'm sure there's nothing to worry about.'

'You sound like you don't believe me, and I know what I saw.'

'I do believe you,' Lorenzo insisted.

'Then act like you do and stop telling me I'm imagining things.'

'Talk me through it again,' Lorenzo said, his voice suggesting his patience was being tested to the limit. 'Perhaps I missed something the first time round.'

'Carlo approached me in the square, then invited me out to lunch.' She looked expectantly at Lorenzo.

'And that's it?' His expression

reflected his impatience.

'You don't find that unusual?'

'Honest answer — no. You were set up to sketch portraits. Carlo asked about you doing a picture of his daughter. It was siesta time. Inviting you out to lunch sounds a perfectly normal thing to do.'

Vanessa bit down her frustration with a grunt of exasperation. 'I'm trying to build up a case here,' she insisted.

'Against whom, Paolo or Carlo? And why? What have they done?'

'I don't know. My head's in a muddle. I thought you'd be able to help.'

'It sounds like you're accusing Carlo and Paolo of art theft for the sake of it. You've got very little to go on, and I would suggest you don't go round voicing these ideas to anyone else. We're in enough trouble as it is.'

Vanessa's shoulders sagged. 'I want to prove my innocence.'

'No one's suggesting you're guilty of anything. But I can put your mind at rest on one thing,' Lorenzo said.

'What?'

'Paolo is who he says he is. I ran a check on him. His family own an olive farm. It has been in the family for generations.'

Vanessa frowned, trying to remember Michelle's exact words. 'I think my sister mentioned that Paolo's father was looking for future investment, and that's why a marriage of convenience had been arranged between Paolo and the daughter of a neighbour.'

'Paolo's father is hardly going to fund his farm by stealing a painting, is he? That's if you were thinking along those lines,' Lorenzo qualified his statement with a logic that Vanessa was beginning to find tedious. She ran a hand through her hair.

'Someone broke into Severino's villa.'

'Agreed.'

'And stole a valuable painting.'

'Agreed.'

'Claudia's ring is still missing, isn't it?'

'Yes.'

'On both occasions when things disappeared, I've been present.'

'Now that isn't true. We don't know when Claudia's ring went missing; and as for the painting, Jolly told us about the incident after it happened. You weren't around on either occasion.'

Vanessa chewed her lip. 'So I'm in the clear?'

'Your innocence was never in doubt, even if Claudia did mention that the last time she remembers seeing her ring was when she was on deck with you and her father, saying goodbye. But there's no way you could have got the ring off her finger without either her or Severino noticing. So it must have gone missing after you left.'

'Giovanni might not see it like that.'

'He's not around to accuse anyone, and we have searched *The Riviera* from top to bottom and found nothing. The guests have now departed, and Giovanni has stood everyone down and gone off to America on business for his father.'

'Where is Claudia now?' Vanessa asked.

'I'm not absolutely sure. Milan or Turin I expect, somewhere like that.'

'Then if Giovanni has left the island and Claudia is in Turin, there really is no reason for me to stay on here.'

'There's every reason,' Lorenzo was quick to contradict her.

'I'm not under island arrest, am I?'

Lorenzo watched a small boat churn through the waters. 'I didn't want to have to tell you this . . . ' he spoke slowly.

Vanessa's chest tightened, causing the expression on Lorenzo's face to change.

'There's no need to look so worried,' he reassured her, then waited an agonisingly long moment before saying, 'Do you remember the night we performed the tango in front of Giovanni's guests?'

Most of what Vanessa could recall

was the pressure of Lorenzo's arm around her waist as he supported her arched back.

'Several of the guests took photos,' Lorenzo carried on, 'and they've been posted on social media.'

He looked as though he needed help with his explanation. Mystified, Vanessa stared back at him.

'With captions — location, date, names.' He paused significantly.

'Naming you as Lorenzo Talbot and me as Michelle Blake?' Vanessa finally got his drift. 'Why didn't you tell me earlier?'

'I couldn't find the right moment.'

'We're back to square one, aren't we? Once the truth gets out, I'm prime suspect again.'

'I don't think it's anything to worry about,' Lorenzo insisted. 'I just thought you ought to know.'

'There's Giovanni to worry about, for a start.'

'He's moved on. The cruise is yesterday's news.'

'The lost ring isn't. It's a valuable piece of jewellery.'

'We are going round in circles,' Lorenzo replied. 'Let's talk about something else. It may clear our heads.'

Vanessa watched flames from small braziers flicker into life as they began to ward off the chill night air for those choosing to dine al fresco. The sound of singing in the distance accompanied by a tambourine grew louder.

'Look out,' Lorenzo warned. 'Students.' He reached into his pocket for some loose change as a young man in a harlequin costume pirouetted towards them, waving a ribbon-bedecked collecting box under their noses. A pretty woman wearing national dress pinned an orchid onto Vanessa's top.

'What's are they collecting for?' Vanessa asked.

'The Wild One,' Lorenzo explained. 'It's what everyone calls the volcano. It hasn't erupted for years, but a charity fund was set up because last time it did it destroyed many buildings, including the college. It was in the direct path of the volcano and couldn't withstand the assault. The authorities decided it mustn't be allowed to happen again.'

Vanessa watched the students singing and dancing their way along the water's edge, wishing she felt as carefree.

'Anyway, no more talk of leaving?' Lorenzo prompted.

'I can't stay on forever.'

'What do you have to go back to?'

Vanessa didn't want to admit that the truth was very little. Since she had injured her ankle, she had found it difficult to settle into a routine. She enjoyed the challenge of change, and dancing on cruise ships had left her with a love of the sun.

'To think it was only a short time ago I was sitting on my houseboat watching the rain bounce off the tow path, wondering if I'd ever see the sun again,' she spoke half to herself.

'And I was invalided out of the police, bad shoulder,' Lorenzo briefly explained, 'wondering what the future held for me. Life can change in an instant.'

'How long have you worked for the Petucci family?' Vanessa asked.

'I don't. I'm freelance, and I think I've reached another life-changing moment. Looking after pampered playboys isn't my scene.'

'What will you do?'

'Nothing for the moment, because we're not finished here yet, are we?'

'We?' Vanessa queried, her mouth dry.

Lorenzo moved in closer towards her. She stiffened. She wasn't sure she had the willpower to resist should he try to kiss her again. The light ebbing from the day was putting on a spectacular display of crimson, orange and scarlet. One or two determined stars were beginning to pinprick through some hazy purple clouds. She could feel the warmth of Lorenzo's body beside hers.

'It's quite something, isn't it?' He looked out towards the horizon. 'An artist's dream. No wonder there are so many painters on the island all striving to capture the moment. How can you bear to even think about leaving?'

Vanessa followed Lorenzo's gaze to where the sun was slipping below the horizon. 'I'll stay on,' she said, not sure where her sudden decision came from.

Lorenzo placed an arm around her shoulder. 'You've made the right choice.' His lips touched her ear as he spoke.

'But I'm not making any promises for the future.'

She tried to convince herself that Severino was the reason for her decision to stay, and Jolly too; but deep down she knew it wasn't true. The thought of life without Lorenzo was growing harder to imagine. But did he feel the same way about her?

14

'I have to go down to the market this morning, and then later I will have lunch with my son,' Jolly announced over breakfast on the terrace. 'Can I leave you to keep an eye on the Maestro?'

'Of course.' Vanessa finished the last of her fresh orange juice.

'He is less tired today, and has expressed the wish that you join him in the studio. He wants to show you *Il Pomeriggio*.' Jolly paused then added, her brown eyes filled with pride, 'It is an honour not bestowed on many.'

Vanessa was touched by the gesture. 'I'm looking forward to seeing it.'

'A word of warning — you must be careful not to touch it.'

'I won't set off the alarm,' Vanessa promised.

'It is not alarmed,' Jolly explained. 'The Maestro will not allow contact for reasons of preservation. Too much exposure to the human touch is not good for the masterpiece.'

'Surely it's more important to have the painting alarmed?'

'I will not have the Maestro or his methods questioned.' Jolly looked outraged at the thought, and Vanessa feared she might have gone too far.

'It makes so much extra work for you,' she tempered down her criticism, 'always having to check up on things in the studio.'

'It is my privilege. We will say no more about it.' Jolly held up a hand, and Vanessa lapsed into silence, not daring to interrupt again. 'The Maestro is getting restless,' Jolly continued, 'so it is good that you should provide a distraction. He will enjoy showing you his works of art.'

'Have you seen *Il Pomeriggio*?'

'Many times.' Jolly's eyes were now filled with mischief. 'You must let me know if you can spot the Maestro's signature.'

'He signs all his work, doesn't he?'

Jolly still looked as though she were enjoying a secret joke. 'There are some who say *Il Pomeriggio* is different.'

'Tell me more.' Vanessa leaned forward eagerly.

'My lips are sealed.' Jolly made a gesture of silence by raising her finger to her lips, her eyes twinkling with amusement. 'Now, how was your evening with Lorenzo?'

'I hope I didn't wake you when I got back.'

At the end of the evening, Lorenzo had walked Vanessa up the hill. From the summit, they could hear the celebrations continuing down in the harbour. Lorenzo had tried to persuade Vanessa to stay on until the music and dancing finished, but she knew how easy it would be to be seduced by Santa Agathe's temptations: sunsets and white sand beaches and a sea the colour of deepest azure. Lorenzo had made no protest when she decided to end their evening early. He was another temptation she knew she had to resist. It was vital for her to remember she was in the middle of a personal drama. This was no time to harbour deeper physical emotions.

Lorenzo hadn't attempted to kiss Vanessa again. After promising to keep in touch, he had made sure she was safely inside the villa security gates before striding back down the hill.

Jolly looked disappointed when she realised Vanessa was not going to reveal further details about her evening with Lorenzo, but she did not pursue the matter.

'I slept well,' Jolly admitted, 'as did the Maestro.'

'Have you heard anything more about *The Harbour at Sunset*?' Vanessa asked.

Jolly shrugged. 'It is gone,' she announced, the flat note in her voice replacing her earlier exuberance. 'We will not see it again.'

'Surely someone in the community must know something.'

'If they do, they have said nothing.' She began to clear away the breakfast things. 'By the way, be prepared,' she warned.

'For what?' Vanessa had to stop herself from looking over her shoulder. She still couldn't shake off the feeling that she was about to be apprehended as a suspect in a jewel robbery.

'The Maestro likes to be the centre of attention. The doctor has refused permission for him to leave the villa, even though it is fiesta week. He does not like this, but he does not dare disobey the doctor. The doctor is my cousin.'

'I see.' Vanessa wasn't exactly sure of the relevance of Jolly's relationship to the doctor, but its significance appeared to carry some weight with Severino.

'You should be grateful,' Jolly insisted. 'The Maestro can be very willful. He will try to hoodwink you into helping him escape for the day, so it is up to you to keep an eye on him. Do not let him get away with the slightest misdemeanour.'

'You're making him sound like a naughty schoolboy.' Vanessa was beginning to wonder what she had taken on. 'I can't stop him leaving his own property, Jolly, if he wants to take a walk or something.'

'You must entertain him.'

'How?'

'Say the right thing. Praise his work. Tell him he is the best painter in the world.'

'Surely he knows that already.'

'Naturally; but like all artists, the Maestro has a huge ego. He needs reassurance.'

'I'll do my best,' Vanessa promised, relieving Jolly of the breakfast tray. She watched the housekeeper wobble off on the treacherous bicycle, then sauntered down to the path to the studio carrying a tray of cold drinks.

The door was flung open as she approached. 'Where have you been? I have been waiting hours for you.' Severino was dressed in a paint-spattered smock and loose black trousers, and his trademark straw hat was perched on his head at an angry angle.

'I've brought you some fresh orange juice.' Remembering Jolly's words, Vanessa did her best to deliver a bright smile. 'Would you like to sit outside, or is the sun too hot for you?'

'Orange juice is horrible stuff. I don't want any.'

Severino turned his back, leaving Vanessa standing uncertainly on the step. As there was no invitation to follow him inside, she cautiously entered the darkened studio. Although the blinds were pulled down, she could see that the walls were a mass of paintings, but standing in pride of place in the middle of the room on a highlighted easel stood *Il Pomeriggio*.

Vanessa placed the tray of drinks on a side table and walked slowly towards it. Unaware that Severino was watching her intently, she held her breath as she stood in front of what had to be one of the most famous paintings in the world.

Severino's beloved wife Maria, Claudia's mother, was engaged in the domestic task of hanging out the washing. Although her head was turned away from the artist, Severino had captured every line of her neck and the curves of her back. Concentrating on her task, she appeared not to have noticed that her blouse had slipped off one of her shoulders, revealing lightly suntanned flesh. The picture aroused such simple emotions that it was impossible not to be affected by the message it conveyed — a young mother performing a simple domestic duty. Yet why were her feet bare and her hair loose? The angle of the sun beating down from a cloudless sky suggested it was early afternoon, but her appearance resembled that of a woman who had only recently woken up. Vanessa blushed at the implication, but the simple dignity of the picture more than compensated for the implied circumstances of her recent activities.

It created questions; it provoked the senses. Vanessa could smell the fresh washing and feel the sunlight on the baked stone courtyard. She was looking at the work of an artistic genius. She had seen copies of the famous masterpiece many times, but nothing had prepared her for the passion of the original. Her fingers itched to get a feel of the canvas. She would have reached out to touch it had Jolly not warned her.

'You like it?'

She had been unaware of Severino standing beside her until he spoke, his voice rough as if daring her to say she hated it. Her throat locked, Vanessa turned to face him.

'There are tears in your eyes,' he said slowly.

'It's beautiful,' she said; then, feeling foolish, she dashed them away with the back of her hand. 'Sorry.'

'There is no need to apologise. Art is for the emotions,' Severino replied. 'And my work has touched your soul?'

Vanessa nodded.

For the first time since she had known Severino, he displayed uncharacteristic modesty by saying softly, 'Your reaction means more to me than all the accolades in the world.' Raising her hand to his lips, his kissed it. 'I apologise for being rude to you earlier. Please put it down to my temperament, and do me the honour of not mentioning it again.'

'I won't,' Vanessa assured him, feeling she was falling under the artist's spell.

'Would you like to see some of my other paintings?' he asked with barely disguised enthusiasm. 'Things are in a bit of a mess, but you don't mind that, do you?'

The studio was compact, but it was crammed with examples of Severino's work. Sketches had been thrust into huge folders and pushed out of the way behind easels displaying his more prominent work. Still in a daze, Vanessa watched him produce half-finished works and preliminary drawings, all portraying life on Santa Agathe.

'I used to do workshops,' he explained, 'but it became too much for me. I was always being approached by big businesses. They wanted me to sponsor their products or allow my work to be used as an advertisement. I turned them all down. Where is the pride in that?'

'Your work is its own advertisement,' Vanessa replied.

'My thoughts exactly. And now I have a confession.'

'You do?'

'Let us enjoy a glass of Jolly's orange juice first. There are sun chairs by the door, and sunshades. Can you see to them for me while I do something to improve my appearance? Apart from the doctor and Jolly, you are my first visitor in days.'

Severino disappeared into his private quarters while Vanessa set about the task of making the patio as comfortable as possible.

'I feel better now.' Severino had made an effort with his hair and changed into clean tunic and trousers. He shaded his eyes against the startling brightness of the sun. 'Every day the light is different,' he explained. 'No two mornings are the same. The sun rises every morning and sets every evening, but in between the world is crammed with different colours, sights, sounds and smells. I try to recreate those images in my work, but after all these years I am still learning.'

He settled down in one of the canvas chairs. Vanessa was pleased to see he was smiling again, his good humour restored.

'You are wondering about my confession?' he said, looking like an eager child waiting to open some birthday presents. 'I have come to a professional decision.'

'Should you be confiding in me?'

Vanessa shifted uncomfortably in her seat.

'Who else is there to tell?'

'Your agent?'

'I don't have one.'

'Claudia?'

'I don't know where she is, and I won't confide in Jolly. She isn't family.'

'Neither am I.'

'But my decision involves you.'

Vanessa now began to feel giddy and wished she'd had the sense to wear her sun hat.

'There's no need to look so worried. I have decided not to go ahead with *La Sera*.'

Vanessa had been clenching her teeth so tightly her mouth hurt, and she wasn't sure she heard Severino correctly.

'*Il Pomeriggio* is unique, wouldn't you say? There is no need for a sequel.'

Vanessa expelled a silent breath of relief.

'Creating a masterpiece takes time, hard work and many hours of trauma, and I'm not sure I could reproduce anything as perfect again, so I have decided I won't even try. You are not disappointed?'

'Not at all,' Vanessa was quick to reassure Severino before he changed his mind.

'These days I find it easier to reflect on past creations. It is I fear a sign of age.' He raised his bushy eyebrows expectantly. Vanessa picked up on his cue.

'It isn't a question of age. You've done the right thing.'

'When I was a young man, I never did the right thing. It stifled the imagination.'

Vanessa sensed that Severino was lapsing back into his bad mood, and his next words confirmed her suspicions.

'You are free to leave the villa whenever you like.'

'Do you want me to leave today?' Vanessa responded in a faint voice, doing her best to come to terms with the sudden twist of events.

'I don't want you to leave at all,' Severino admitted. 'But I think perhaps it would be for the best, don't you?'

'Has Claudia said something?' Vanessa felt compelled to ask.

'I don't think so, but she will return home for Jolly's birthday. She never misses it. You must stay on as well. After that you can leave.' Severino spoke as if everything had already been arranged. 'Although Jolly insists she doesn't want a fuss, she is not telling the truth. We invite everyone and have a feast and it never rains. You know — ' Severino smiled at the memory. ' — one year the Wild One had a touch of indigestion. Some of the guests were nervous, but our party soon put a stop to any volcanic nonsense. The Wild One calmed down and we got on with our celebrations.'

'Will Giovanni Petucci be coming to the party with Claudia?' Vanessa asked, privately thinking it might be a good idea for her to invent an excuse to vacate the island before Jolly's party.

A shadow crossed Severino's face. 'I am not sure. He is a very busy man.'

'That's a pity.' Vanessa felt a wave of relief.

'I don't mind about that, but what I do mind is the way he treats my daughter. His father is a big man, very important. Claudia is from the island. She is a simple girl with simple values. She does not need a huge great token of affection from the man who loves her.'

'You mean her engagement ring?' Vanessa spoke carefully.

'It is an atrocity.' He shuddered. 'So vulgar. But it doesn't matter, does it? Someone has had the sense to steal it. I hope they throw it away; hurl it into the sea, where it belongs. Let's not waste any more time talking about the Petucci family,' Severino insisted. 'Shall we go for a little walk?'

'Jolly told me the doctor forbade you from leaving the villa.'

There was a faint look of disgust on

Severino's face. 'Nobody forbids me to do anything.'

Fearing another mercurial change of temperament, Vanessa suggested, 'Why don't you tell me more about your paintings?'

'I don't want to.' Severino sounded like a sulky child.

'I've heard . . . ' Vanessa shook her head. 'No, you're right.' She couldn't resist casting a sly glance in Severino's direction. Her ruse had worked, and she now had his full attention.

'What have you heard?' he demanded.

'It's probably only a rumour,' she began, 'about your famous signature.'

'I will set you a challenge,' Severino interrupted, his good humour restored, 'and you have until Jolly's birthday party to come up with the answer.'

'I may not be here,' Vanessa hedged.

'You will be here,' Severino replied in a tone of voice that brooked no argument.

'How can you be sure?'

'Because I have said so.'

Vanessa opened her mouth to protest, then decided it wouldn't be a wise move to go against Severino's wishes.

'What is this challenge?' she asked.

'It has defeated everyone who has ever undertaken it.'

'What makes you think I'll succeed?'

Severino was all smiles again. 'Because you let tears trickle down your face the first time you viewed *Il Pomeriggio*,' he replied.

Vanessa lowered her gaze to the sun-baked flagstones.

'The challenge is,' she heard Severino announce through a haze of embarrassment mixed with curiosity, 'to find out whether the rumour you have heard about my signature on *Il Pomeriggio* is true.'

15

'Divers discovered a wrecked ship here last summer.'

Lorenzo and Vanessa stood side by side on the summit of the cliffs surrounding Santa Agathe and looked down into a barely visible inlet tucked away under their shadow. Vanessa did her best to concentrate, but her mind was wandering away from the sweeping beauty of the remote bay below them.

'It lay undiscovered on the seabed for years,' Lorenzo carried on with his explanation.

Despite the heat of the day, Vanessa shuddered at the thought of the lives lost. Today the sea looked calm and untroubled and gave every appearance of being man's best friend. Santa Agathe — the island of magic; yet the sea and the ever-brooding Wild One were clouds on its horizon, both beautiful and destructive. Vanessa winced as she turned too quickly. A sharp stab of pain shot up her ankle.

'Do you want to rest up?' Lorenzo shaded his eyes against the bright sun and indicated a rocky outcrop behind them. 'Over there?'

Vanessa rubbed her ankle.

'Lean on me.' He held out his arm.

'It's only a twinge,' she insisted, reluctant to take up Lorenzo's offer of help. Limping across to the sun-warmed rock, she sank down on a smooth slab. It had been a long climb to the summit, but feeling the need for exercise, she had agreed to Lorenzo's suggestion that they visit the ruins of one of the first settlements on Santa Agathe.

'You don't want it swelling up, otherwise you may never dance the tango again,' Lorenzo joked as he sat down beside her.

'I never did thank you properly, did I?' Vanessa sipped some mineral water from the small bottle he had produced.

'For standing in for Paolo?'

He leaned back against the outcrop. 'I don't think you did.'

'Your sisters did a good job teaching you to dance.'

'Next time I see them I must remember to tell them that our Sunday afternoons in the lounge weren't wasted.'

'Your sisters don't live on Santa Agathe?'

'Julie lives in a huge rectory on the East Anglia coast with her husband and two children. Deborah does something arty in a caravan. We meet up from time to time; once a year is usually enough. They can get incredibly bossy with their little brother, so I limit my visits.'

'Do they never visit the island?'

'The family used to have a holiday villa here, but we sold up when our parents died.'

All the time he was talking, Vanessa continued to rub her ankle.

'I'm very good at massage if it's still giving you trouble,' Lorenzo offered.

'It's fine,' Vanessa assured him.

A group of ramblers ambled past, and some art students set up school further along the outcrop.

'In that case, down to business,' he said. 'Why the early-morning telephone call, and why couldn't we meet at the villa?'

'I didn't want to upset Jolly or Severino.'

'Have there been developments?'

'Carlo's been hanging around the villa,' Vanessa said. 'I saw him yesterday afternoon.'

After her morning spent with Severino, Vanessa had left the artist to enjoy his siesta while she returned to her room in the villa to start making arrangements to return home. Her heart had been heavy at the prospect of leaving the island, but with Severino abandoning plans for La Sera, there was no reason for her to stay. Lost in thought, she had glanced out of one of the upstairs windows.

'What was he doing?' Lorenzo asked.

'Standing by the gates and peering down the drive.'

'Perhaps he's a fan of Severino's.'

'What on earth could he see from the end of the drive?'

'What do you think he was up to?'

'I don't know, but you've got to admit it's suspicious.'

'The islanders like to know what's going on. The fiesta always creates extra interest.'

'I just wish Severino and Jolly would take security more seriously. I love them both dearly, but they would try the patience of a saint. Anyone can walk into Severino's studio if they've a mind to it. He leaves the doors wide open because he says canvases need to breathe. *Il Pomeriggio* is on full display, and we know he disconnects the alarms — and have you seen the wall surrounding the back of the villa? It's falling down in places. It wouldn't keep a child out.'

'You need to confront Carlo. Ask him why he was talking to Paolo. Say you saw him outside Severino's villa. See what he comes up with.'

'Supposing he asks why I didn't speak to Paolo? After all, he is my brother-in-law.'

'You could say you weren't certain it was Paolo. You've only met him once, haven't you?'

'It might work.'

'Give it a try,' Lorenzo urged. 'I would hate something to happen to Severino because we sat back and did nothing.'

'I'm due to see Carlo this afternoon after Assunta gets out of school. We need to do a final sitting for her picture.'

Lorenzo picked up a small stone and held it in his hand thoughtfully. 'Talking of artwork, what did you think of *Il Pomeriggio*?' He glanced enquiringly at Vanessa. A dreamy look came into her eyes, turning them a hazy smoky blue. Her pale skin was now lightly bronzed; and as her generous mouth curved into a smile, two stragglers from the rambling group returned it with a friendly wave and called out a greeting.

'What did they say?' Vanessa asked Lorenzo.

'They think we are lovers and they're wishing us every happiness for the future.'

Vanessa jerked upright.

'Mind your ankle,' Lorenzo cautioned.

'Tell them they're wrong,' she hissed.

'You tell them.'

'I don't speak the language.'

'Everyone understands English, and if you carry on looking so cross you'll make things worse. They'll think we're having a lovers' tiff.'

'For goodness sake, you're enjoying this, aren't you?'

'I am, actually. It's a lovely day, so why don't you relax? Tell me about *Il Pomeriggio*.'

'I don't know where to start,' Vanessa admitted.

'First impressions?'

She took a deep breath. 'It controls

your emotions. It makes you sad, happy, curious. It talks to you.'

'At last.' Lorenzo leaned forward.

'At last what?' Vanessa wished she could move away from his touch, but the warmth of his fingers on her flesh eased the throbbing in her ankle.

'Santa Agathe has softened you up. The old lady had her hands full with you, didn't she?'

'You asked me what I thought of Severino's work. It's got nothing to do with Santa Agathe or island magic.'

'Don't let the Wild One hear you.'

'Severino didn't spout any nonsense about magic or volcanoes. He took my pleasure in his work as a compliment.'

'He would. All artists are vain.'

'That's not fair. He's brilliant.'

'I agree, but it doesn't stop him using his brilliance to his own advantage.'

Vanessa lapsed into silent agreement with Lorenzo.

'Did he set you the challenge?' Lorenzo asked. 'The one about his signature?'

'You've heard it?' Vanessa was disappointed.

'Everyone on the island knows about it. At one time or another they've all undertaken the challenge.'

'Why does he do it?'

'Severino's got very little time for art critics, amateur or professional, and he says things to provoke people for the sheer fun of it. I think in the beginning he did it to get his work noticed, then it sort of gained momentum. He's not as unworldly as he appears, and there's no such thing as bad publicity. *Il Pomeriggio*'s signature is supposed to be different in some way from the rest of his work.'

'I didn't spot anything,' Vanessa mumbled.

'Neither has anyone else, so I shouldn't let it bother you. By the way, have you heard the latest?'

'What now?'

'The engagement is off.'

'What?'

'That's if social media is to be believed. Claudia and Giovanni are giving out all the usual reasons — global lifestyle, artistic differences, that sort of thing. And whilst they have the greatest respect for each other, they feel their life paths are going in opposite directions, and that it's better to part while they are still friends.'

'Do you believe them?'

'I'm not sure what to believe, but that's the official version.'

'What about the ring?' Vanessa asked.

'The trail's gone cold.'

Vanessa eased her leg away from Lorenzo's fingers. 'I hope Claudia isn't too upset.'

'I don't think Severino will be,' Lorenzo said. 'Cruises on private yachts aren't his thing.'

'At least Giovanni won't be attending Jolly's birthday party.' Vanessa scrambled to a seated position. 'I nearly forgot.' She produced a crumpled card from the pocket of her crops.

'What is it?'

'Your invitation to Jolly's birthday party.'

'I'm honoured.'

'You're not allowed to refuse.'

'I wouldn't dream of it.'

'It's the highlight of the summer season at the Villa Amoretti. Claudia always flies home for it.' Vanessa paused. 'Is something else bothering you?'

Lorenzo frowned at her, and she knew she couldn't put off telling him any longer.

'Severino isn't going ahead with his plans for a sequel to *Il Pomeriggio*. He's said I'm free to leave the villa after Jolly's party.'

She held her breath, wondering what Lorenzo's reaction would be; but before either of them could speak, her mobile signalled an incoming message.

'Don't answer it,' Lorenzo snapped.

'It's from Michelle.' Vanessa raised her eyes to meet his. 'She's pregnant.'

*   *   *

226

'It's absolutely perfect. You've captured Assunta's likeness so well. My mother will be so pleased with her present. You are looking forward to the party?'

Vanessa looked to where Carlo's daughter was busy playing tag with Mauricio's grandson in the main square. Something in the way Assunta's dark brown eyes sparkled with amusement struck a chord at the back of Vanessa's mind.

'Jolly is your mother?' she queried slowly as things now became clear to her.

How could Vanessa not have realised earlier? Carlo had even introduced himself as Carlo Boniface and been clearly disappointed when she hadn't recognised him.

'I am sorry for all the secrecy,' Carlo apologised, 'but I didn't want you inadvertently spoiling my surprise. I did wonder if you might make the connection when I told you my name was Boniface, but when you didn't, I decided not to enlighten you.'

'I'm so pleased you're Jolly's son.'

Carlo looked confused. 'You are? Why?'

'Because I saw you outside the villa yesterday afternoon.'

'Saying goodbye to my mother, yes.'

'And you know all about the view from the terrace and Severino's paintings.'

'Naturally. I have been there many times.'

Awash with shame, Vanessa began to fold up her easel. 'Can you tell me why you were talking to Paolo Vargas?' she asked.

'Who?' Carlo continued to look puzzled.

'When we had lunch together, you were talking to a man in the square.'

'Paolo, is that his name? Do you know him?'

'He's married to my sister.'

'He is your brother-in-law?' Carlo's confusion deepened. 'Why didn't you join us?'

More shame washed over Vanessa as she tried to come to terms with her unfounded suspicions about Carlo. 'I thought you were having a private conversation.' It was a lame excuse, but the best she could come up with at short notice.

'Someone had told him my mother works for Severino, and he wanted an introduction to Giovanni Petucci. He was disappointed when I told him I couldn't help. I don't really know Giovanni, and anyway, according to my mother he's no longer on the island.'

'Do you know why Paolo was on Santa Agathe and not with my sister?'

'I'm sorry, I don't. If you're ready to leave, I will carry your things for you. Assunta,' he called out to his daughter, 'come along.'

As they struggled up the last part of the hill to the villa, Vanessa heard a vehicle draw up behind them. Assunta let out an ear-piercing shriek and raced towards the taxi.

'Steady,' Carlo called after his daughter as someone opened the passenger door.

'Darling.' Claudia dropped her packages and held open her arms. 'How are you?'

Scooping the child up in her arms, she twirled Assunta round, only coming to a halt when she collided with Carlo. With scant regard for the contents of Vanessa's canvas bag, he dropped it on the ground and locked his arms around the two of them, kissing Claudia on the cheek. Standing to one side, Vanessa began to feel uncomfortably in the way until Claudia caught sight of her over Carlo's shoulder and pushed him away.

'I am sorry.' She came forward and kissed Vanessa on the cheek. 'Where are my manners? It's lovely to see you again, Michelle.'

16

'Why did you pretend to be your sister?' Jolly asked, a distinctly chilly note in her voice.

Claudia's unscheduled arrival had created chaos; and when she had addressed Vanessa as Michelle, Carlo had corrected Claudia, but there hadn't been time to explain. All Vanessa had managed was a whispered 'Michelle is my sister. I'll tell you later' to Jolly, who was now demanding to know full details of the subterfuge.

'It's complicated,' Vanessa admitted.

'Is it to do with a man?'

'In a roundabout way.'

'The Maestro won't be pleased when he learns of the deception.'

'Actually he already knows about it,' Vanessa confessed.

'You have told him?'

'He didn't seem too fussed,' Vanessa

reassured her. 'It was a simple misunderstanding. Michelle is my sister.'

'So you've already told me. I do not need to know the details,' Jolly said brushing the incident away with a preoccupied air. 'I'm sure you had your reasons. We have more serious things to discuss.'

'Severino hasn't had a setback? There hasn't been another break-in?' Vanessa asked with a pang of concern. She had been away from the villa all day, first with Lorenzo then Carlo. 'I shouldn't have left you alone with Severino for such a long time. I'm sorry.'

'The Maestro is fine, and overjoyed that his daughter has arrived early for my birthday party. He will now have the person he loves most in this world here to look after him.'

'I know. Severino has informed me I have to leave,' Vanessa began, wondering why Jolly was being so chilly towards her.

Jolly continued, not listening to Vanessa. 'Miss Claudia has her own life

232

to lead. The Maestro knows that, but he still would like her to settle on the island and provide him with grandchildren.'

'Are you saying you want me to leave immediately now that Claudia's returned to the villa?'

'What I need from you, Vanessa, is your promise that you will not go for any more secret walks with my son.'

'Secret walks?' Vanessa frowned, feeling as though a rug had been pulled from underneath her feet.

'I saw you spying on him from the window when he was in the road outside, and I know of your meetings in the main square, and that he takes you out to lunch.'

'What?'

'You cannot deny anything. Assunta told me all about it. She called you the lovely lady with the golden hair.'

'Jolly,' Vanessa raised her voice as the housekeeper seemed in no mood to listen to her explanation, 'Carlo took me to lunch once.'

'Why did he do that?'

'It was the siesta hour.'

'You contradict yourself,' Jolly protested. 'If you hardly know my son, why would he take you out for lunch?'

'It was for business reasons,' Vanessa stuttered out an explanation.

'You are blushing. I do not believe you.'

'Jolly, I'm telling the truth. Ask Carlo.'

'I cannot. He and Claudia have gone out to visit friends, then they are going to have dinner together.' She paused. 'You are not jealous?'

'Why should I be?'

'Carlo and Claudia have known each other a long time. Claudia was at school with Patricia his wife. She is godmother to Assunta.'

'I see,' Vanessa said, although she was still mystified as to exactly what was upsetting Jolly.

'I do not like the way men are attracted to you, Vanessa. I do not say you encourage them, but there will be trouble if you go on like this.'

'I beg your pardon?' Vanessa gaped.

'Why are you not content with your Lorenzo?'

'I am. I mean, he's not my Lorenzo. Jolly, what's this all about?'

'And the other one?' There was a mutinous look on Jolly's face.

'What other one?'

'The one who came to the villa asking for you?'

'I don't know any other men on the island.'

'He knows you. I told him you were not here, and he seemed very disappointed not to see you.'

'Did he leave a name?'

'Paolo.'

Vanessa gasped. 'Paolo was here?'

'Ah, I was right.' Jolly folded her arms in confrontation. 'You do know him. It is useless to deny anything. I can see from the expression on your face you and this Paolo are friends.'

'Jolly, Paolo is my brother-in-law. He's married to my sister, Michelle, the one I was telling you about.'

'The one you impersonated?' Jolly wasn't smiling, but she no longer sounded so upset.

'And,' Vanessa went on, 'I've just learned my sister is expecting a baby.'

This last piece of news caused the scowl to finally leave Jolly's face, to be replaced by a tentative smile. 'A baby? That is good news. You are going to be an aunt for the first time?'

'I am, and I promise to behave like one. So you see, your fears about my love life are unfounded.'

Jolly sat down on a wooden chair with a heavy thump. 'I am sorry. I should have trusted you, and I should have told you earlier that your brother-in-law Paolo was here, but I was suspicious of you and Carlo. I would not have believed what Assunta was saying about you, but I saw you looking out the window to where Carlo was standing. It was such odd behaviour.'

'I was wondering what he was doing here. I didn't realise he was your son.

Then when he seemed to know an awful lot about the villa . . . ' It was Vanessa's turn to feel embarrassed. 'There have been break-ins.'

'You took my Carlo for an art thief?' Jolly's maternal outrage resurfaced.

'No, I didn't.'

'How could you?'

'I'm sorry. I was only thinking of you and Severino.'

'Pah. The Maestro and I can look after ourselves. We don't need your help.'

'Jolly, can we start again if I promise there's nothing of a romantic nature between myself and Carlo, and that I no longer suspect him of wanting to break into the villa?'

'I don't know if I can trust you.'

Vanessa took hold of Jolly's work-roughened hand. 'I don't want to lose your friendship. It means so much to me, and I thought you liked me too.'

'I have something in my eye,' Jolly insisted, dabbing at her face with the corner of her sleeve. 'You are right.' She raised her head and sniffed loudly, then coughed. 'We have both made mistakes. We will say no more about it.'

Vanessa, who had been holding her breath, let out a sigh of relief. The sturdy ticking of the kitchen clock provided an everyday comforting background. She waited for Jolly to make the first move.

'You have heard that Giovanni Petucci is no longer engaged to Claudia?' Jolly asked after the clock had ticked a full minute away.

'Lorenzo told me.'

'I would so much like Claudia and Carlo to deepen their relationship. The Maestro would like it too, I think.'

'If that's what was worrying you, Jolly,' Vanessa said, feeling a weight lift from her shoulders, understanding now why the housekeeper had acted so out of character, 'I wouldn't dream of standing in their way. You have my word on that. And when you do find out the reason why Carlo took me out to lunch, you'll be pleasantly surprised.'

'Is it to do with my birthday?' Jolly's eyes lit up. 'Carlo always makes a fuss of me. I know it's silly at my age, but it's something I look forward to every year.'

'You're going to have to contain your excitement a little longer.'

'If I cannot squeeze the secret out of you, I suppose I must.' Jolly looked disappointed. 'It's lucky I have other things to take my mind off birthday presents. The weather will be beautiful, and I don't have to do any work. All those who are invited bring a dish, and we put the food on wooden tables, then tell everyone to tuck in. It is a good idea?'

'Very good.'

'I have another good idea. After Assunta has had her bath and gone to bed, why don't we have a supper on our own?'

'What about Severino?'

'He is having a sleep now because Carlo has promised to collect him later. He and Claudia will take him out to supper at his favourite trattoria. I told you my son was a good boy.'

Jolly bustled off, leaving Vanessa still sitting at the kitchen table and feeling drained by all the recent drama. She didn't welcome the sound of her mobile interrupting the silence, but when she saw the caller identity she knew she had to answer it.

'Nessa?' Michelle sounded her usual exuberant self. 'Did you get my message?'

'Yes, I — '

'I'm sorry I couldn't tell you earlier, but I wasn't sure of my condition. That's why I denied being pregnant. Now that it's been confirmed, I'm going public, and you're among the first to know. Isn't it wonderful?'

'Congratulations.'

'I knew you'd be pleased.'

'How did Paolo's family take the news?'

'They're very happy, and they don't mind about us getting married in secret. Nessa, you must get married too. It's the best thing in the world to have a husband who loves you.'

'I'm sure it is.'

'I love all Paolo's sisters to death, and his mother won't let me lift a finger. And better still, it was only a false alarm with his grandmother. She has occasional dizzy spells, but she's made a full recovery. I don't know why I was so scared of meeting them all. Nessa, the farm is wonderful. There are hundreds of cousins and nieces and nephews. You absolutely have to visit. It's the most wonderful place in the world. The sun never stops shining. It's so different from the rain at home.'

Vanessa smiled to herself. As usual, her sister appeared to have gone over the top.

'Paolo told me he tried to contact you when he flew back to the island, but a scary lady at your villa frightened him off.'

'I'm sorry I missed him.'

'I would have visited with him, but the doctor said I wasn't to fly for the moment. Something to do with my blood pressure. I couldn't understand everything he said. I'm learning the local language, but it's slow going. Everyone keeps laughing at my mistakes.'

'I'm glad things have worked out for you.'

'What about you?'

'I'm fine.'

'Did you know Giovanni and Claudia have parted company and that *The Riviera* has been closed up and everyone's left? It's such a pity,' Michelle raced on, not waiting for Vanessa's reply. 'Paolo so wanted to get an introduction to Giovanni. He tried some local contacts but without success. His father thought the Petucci family might be interested in investing in the olive farm, so immediately we arrived here he sent Paolo straight back to Santa Agathe. Paolo didn't really want to leave me alone here without him for longer than he had to, so that's why he couldn't stay around to make contact with you. But he does send his love.'

'I understand.'

'You do like him don't you, Nessa?'

'Of course.'

'Then you'll come and visit?' she pleaded.

'As soon as I can,' Vanessa assured her sister.

'Have they found Claudia's ring?'

'Not as yet.'

'That's a pity.'

Vanessa heard the murmur of voices in the background.

'I have to go, Nessa. One of Paolo's sisters wants to introduce me to her cousin. Let me know when you're going to visit, and bring Lorenzo,' she said.

Before Vanessa could reply, the connection was severed. She was still staring at her handset when she heard a voice behind her.

'Jolly said I would find you here.'

Vanessa spun round to face Lorenzo.

'I came to find out how you got on

with Carlo, and Jolly insisted I join you for supper.'

'I should imagine she was delighted to see you.'

'She was over the moon. What's going on?'

'She thought I had a thing going with Carlo, who happens to be her son.'

'No kidding?'

'Claudia's turned up early for Jolly's party. We all bumped into each other outside the villa. Anyway, as the engagement to Giovanni is no longer an issue, she's hoping Carlo and Claudia will get together and eventually provide her and Severino with grandchildren.' Vanessa ticked off the explanations on her fingers. 'Paolo was talking to Carlo because he thought he could get him an introduction to Giovanni, and Paolo was here without Michelle because she can't fly due to her condition. Paolo called in at the villa to see me, but I was out. Jolly turned him away because she thought he was another of my admirers. We've both apologised to each other, and we're best friends again. I don't think I've left anything out, but feel free to ask questions.'

'I think I got most of that, but I don't suppose you'd like to run it past me again?' Lorenzo asked hopefully.

'Not really.' Vanessa expelled another sigh. 'I've only just got my head round it myself.'

'Thought you'd say that. Right, what do you want me to do?'

'We're eating al fresco on the terrace. Jolly's been looking out the party bits and pieces and says we can use paper plates; that way we can save on the washing up. We've got plastic cups too. You don't mind drinking wine out of a plastic cup?'

'I think I can live with that,' Lorenzo replied.

With the lights twinkling in the harbour and nobody able to eat another morsel, Jolly began clearing away, stashing their paper plates in a disposable sack.

'I'll put the bag in the bin for you,

Jolly, if you want to go and check on Assunta,' Lorenzo said, relieving her of her burden.

'Thank you; it is heavy. And if you would go down to the studio and attend to the alarm system for me, Vanessa?'

'What about Severino? We don't want him setting it off accidentally when he gets back.'

'He will have Claudia with him. Normally I would not bother with the alarm until the Maestro has retired for the night, but Claudia does like it to be set while her father is out, even if it is only locally with her. You will find the code and details of what to do in the little table by the front door.'

'I'll join you in a minute,' Lorenzo called after Vanessa.

Vanessa pushed open the studio door and fumbled for the light switch. The sound of students celebrating fiesta night drifted up from the harbour, and she hoped a breakaway group wasn't planning to pay Severino an unscheduled visit. He was their hero, and for most of them their goal was to get a glimpse of *Il Pomeriggio*.

She pulled at the drawer to the table, but it jammed as she tried to release the catch. Bending down, she eased the obstruction before she spotted another object wedged behind the paperwork at the back. Reaching inside, her fingers closed over something small and hard. Careful not to scrape her knuckles, she gently lifted it out.

'What have you got there?' Lorenzo stood in the studio doorway behind her.

Nestled in the palm of Vanessa's hand was a white gold diamond and aquamarine engagement ring.

17

The two of them stared at each other in a shocked silence that was swiftly broken by the sound of footsteps approaching down the pathway.

'Who's there?' a voice called out.

'What do we do?' There was panic in Vanessa's voice.

'Give it to me.' Lorenzo held out his hand.

Vanessa's hesitation caused the moment to be lost. Carlo poked his head round the doorway, his concerned expression replaced with a relieved smile.

'Thank heavens it's only you. We thought Severino might have had another break-in.'

'Lorenzo?' Claudia now appeared beside Carlo. 'And Michelle? What are you doing here?'

'Her name's not Michelle,' Carlo

248

corrected her. 'I told you, it's Vanessa.'

Claudia's eyes narrowed. 'What exactly is going on?'

'Vanessa has been staying at the villa,' Carlo said, 'as company for Severino and my mother.'

Claudia silenced him with a look.

'We came to set the alarm,' Lorenzo began to explain.

'It was set before we left. I did it myself when we collected Papa to take him out to dinner.'

'We didn't know that,' Vanessa put in.

Claudia's eyes swung in her direction. 'What is that you are trying to hide behind your back, Michelle? I mean Vanessa, or whatever your real name is?'

'It's Vanessa.'

Before she could say any more, Claudia lurched forward as further disruption in the doorway caused her to lose her balance. Severino, manhandling a painting, struggled into the studio.

'Here, let me.' Carlo sprang forward to relieve him of his burden. 'You should have left it outside. I would have brought it in for you.'

'It's my painting and I can manage,' Severino insisted.

'No you can't,' a distracted Claudia intervened. 'Don't argue. And do as Carlo says please, Papa.'

Grumbling, Severino relinquished his hold on the canvas; then, spying Vanessa, moved towards her and enveloped her in his open arms, embracing her warmly. 'Good news, Vanessa.' His suntanned face was wreathed in smiles. 'I have found *The Harbour at Sunset*. Here it is. Safe at home again where it belongs.'

'You wouldn't believe where it was,' Carlo began, but got no further, as Severino interrupted him.

'It's my story,' he said.

'Sorry, Maestro,' Carlo backtracked. 'Carry on.'

Severino made sure all eyes were on him before announcing, 'It was propped up against the bar in one of the cafés, on full display.'

'We were strolling by outside, taking the air,' Carlo said, seemingly determined to have his say, 'and only caught sight of it by accident.'

'What was it doing in a café?' Vanessa asked.

'A very good question,' Severino said, nodding. 'Some students came up with the idea to appropriate it for charity purposes. They knew I would never agree to it leaving the villa, so they temporarily borrowed it.'

'Without your permission,' Claudia now intervened.

'They were charging customers to look at it, all proceeds to go to the Wild One fund,' Carlo broke into Severino's explanation again.

'Full marks for initiative, wouldn't you say? And how could I complain?' Severino appealed to Vanessa.

'You couldn't,' she agreed.

'They had collected a lot of money. Of course they were full of apologies, and I insisted they must not do such a thing ever again. But after I signed a few postcards of my paintings for their appeal, we had a party, and everyone is now friends.'

Vanessa looked down to where Carlo had wedged the painting against a packing case.

'You have not seen it before, have you?' Severino said, coming to stand beside her. 'See the patterns the dying sun made on the water? It took me months to get them right. Even now I am not sure I have captured the character of the moment. It is so difficult to get these things just how you want them.'

Vanessa knew she was in the company of artistic genius, but it was not the moment to praise Severino in front of his daughter.

'No tears?' Severino looked disappointed. 'Vanessa is an art connoisseur,' he informed Claudia.

'Really?' She arched an eyebrow.

'After *Il Pomeriggio*,' Severino said, turning back to Vanessa, 'this is my favourite work. The students recognised this. They told me they did not dare interfere with my masterpiece, so they took my second best work of art.'

'That's hardly something to be proud of,' Claudia insisted. 'They broke the law.'

Severino stifled a yawn. 'My darling girl, I am not going to prosecute anyone. Everyone profited by their actions, so it would be mean-spirited of me to send them to jail.'

Claudia tried to reason with her father. 'All I'm saying is, they can't go around taking things when the mood is on them.'

'You are probably right, as always.' Severino's eyelids began to droop. 'I won't argue with you. I always lose,' he added, looking at Vanessa with the suggestion of a wink.

'Papa,' Claudia reproached him, 'why did you not let me bring you home earlier?'

'Because I was having such a good time.'

'You are exhausted.'

'I am rather tired,' he agreed.

'You must go to bed immediately.'

Severino pulled a face. 'There was a time not so very long ago when I said the very same thing to you, my darling.'

'Now the position is reversed.' The tone of Claudia's voice suggested she was well used to having this type of conversation with her father. 'You wouldn't want to miss Jolly's special day, would you, because you had overdone the partying?'

'I've never missed a party in my life,' Severino protested.

'You are not a young man anymore, Papa. You can't stay up all night like you used to.'

'A sad fact,' he agreed, 'but true.'

Claudia's face softened as she kissed Severino's forehead. 'Now say good night to everyone.'

Severino looked about to protest, then changed his mind. 'Lovely as it is to see you all, I think I must do as my daughter says,' he admitted. 'Claudia, will you put *The Harbour* back in its rightful place, and we'll say no more about it?'

'I will,' she assured him. 'Now off you go.'

'You know, the students said it was very easy to break in to the studio,' Severino confided to Lorenzo, 'I really am going to have to do something about my security. Perhaps you can help?'

'We'll talk about it in the morning,' Lorenzo assured him.

'Then good night, sweet ladies.' He smiled and blew a kiss to Claudia and Vanessa. 'Pleasant dreams, and to the gentlemen too,' he added.

'I should be on my way as well,' Carlo excused himself. 'It's been quite a night. When word got round that Severino was in town, everyone wanted a piece of him, and he's not one to shy away from the attention.'

'You don't have to tell me,' Claudia replied.

'I'll go check on Assunta and then say good night to my mother. See you all at the party.' He cast Vanessa a meaningful look that was not lost on Claudia. 'If not before.'

No one moved until his footsteps faded into the distance.

'Would you like some help replacing Severino's painting?' Lorenzo asked.

'Thank you, I can manage.' Claudia swept past them without a look at Vanessa.

'We'd better follow her,' Lorenzo said.

'What are we going to do about our find?' Vanessa hissed, still clutching the ring.

'I'm pretty sure it is Claudia's engagement ring, but I suppose we should check it out first.'

'If it is, how did it get into Severino's studio?'

'I have no idea.'

'You don't think I put it there, do you?'

'Did you?'

'Of course I didn't. I found it when I was looking for the security code moments before you discovered me with it in my hand.' Vanessa glared at Lorenzo.

'Only checking base. Don't fly off the handle. I need to be prepared. Claudia says she set the alarm before they all went out to dinner, remember?'

'Jolly asked me to set it. You heard her.'

'Come on.' Lorenzo tugged at Vanessa's arm. 'We can't hang around arguing about it out here. Best get it over with.'

Claudia was standing at the big picture window, staring out at the view below. There were dark circles under her eyes, and she looked as though she were in need of a good night's sleep. Vanessa also noted she had lost weight. Her dress hung loosely on her hips.

'I think we all owe each other an explanation.' She turned slowly as Vanessa and Lorenzo entered the main studio. 'I'm not sure I know where to start, so perhaps you'd like to go first, er Vanessa?'

'Michelle is my younger sister.'

'I see.' From the tone of Claudia's voice, it was obvious she was merely being polite.

'For personal reasons,' Vanessa ploughed on, 'Michelle was unable to fulfil her engagement on *The Riviera*, so I took her place.'

'And you knew about this?' Claudia looked at Lorenzo.

'It was my suggestion,' he admitted.

'Why did you suggest such a thing?'

'There wasn't time to perform the necessary security checks for Vanessa. Everything had been made out in Michelle's name, so we came to an agreement.'

'To deceive Giovanni?'

'No,' Vanessa protested.

'You don't call assuming your sister's identity a deception?'

'No. Well yes, but I only did it because it was such an important occasion. When I originally promised to stand in for Michelle, I didn't realise there would be complications, and by the time I did it was too late to back out.'

'I suppose I can follow your logic.' Claudia looked as though she was losing interest in Vanessa's explanation. 'Tell me,' she enquired with a smile that resembled Severino's, 'was the tango with Lorenzo part of the deal?'

'That was my idea,' Vanessa admitted. 'I accept full responsibility for everything; and if you want to go telling tales to Giovanni, then you're free to do so. However, I don't know what you and your father have been up to, but I'm not taking the blame for stealing your wretched ring.'

Claudia took a step backwards in alarm, as if scared that Vanessa was going to attack her. Vanessa unclenched her fingers.

'You wanted to know what I was hiding from you? Well here it is.' The stones sparkled in the palm of her hand. 'This is your engagement ring, isn't it? The one that went missing and caused all the fuss?'

'Yes, it is,' admitted Claudia in a hollow voice. 'Have you had it all the time?'

'You know I haven't.'

'Where did you find it?' Claudia looked as though she didn't want to know the answer.

'In the small table by the door.'

'I see.'

'Can you explain how it got there? The last time I saw it, you were wearing it on the day Severino and I disembarked together from *The Riviera*.'

Claudia took the ring out of Vanessa's hand, holding it between her fingers as if it was something unpleasant. 'It's not a nice ring, is it? I never really liked it, but it was Giovanni's choice. He insisted we had to have it.' She now rolled it around the palm of her hand with an expression of distaste on her face.

'I was sorry to hear about your broken engagement,' Lorenzo sympathised.

Claudia raised her eyes towards him.

'Thank you,' was her automatic response.

'Was it because of the missing ring?' he asked.

'Giovanni was very annoyed when he learned I had lost it. But if you must know, the real reason we broke off our engagement was because I knew Giovanni wasn't ready to settle down. Perhaps in a year or two he will have grown up a bit. But — ' Claudia tossed back her head, ' — we weren't suited. I realised it the night we got engaged, but I was backed into a corner. He had invited several of his father's friends to the party. Like you, Vanessa, I felt I could not disappoint everyone.' She paused. 'And there's something else.'

'Go on,' Lorenzo urged.

'My father did not approve of my choice. He would never have openly criticised Giovanni had we got married, but I knew he felt he wasn't the man for me. When the ring disappeared, I had my suspicions that Severino might have slipped it off my finger when he hugged me before we said goodbye. Of course I could not accuse my father.' Claudia shrugged.

'So you let everyone believe it was me?' Vanessa did her best to contain her outrage.

'I had no idea you would get the blame, Vanessa. I didn't even know you weren't the real Michelle Blake. How could I? Had I realised you were implicated, I would never have let you be accused. I am sorry.'

'No one accused Vanessa of anything,' Lorenzo said.

'You insisted I had to clear my name,' Vanessa retaliated.

'That was for your own sake.'

'And just now out there — ' Vanessa gestured to the table by the door. ' — you asked me if I'd put the ring in the table.'

'I didn't for one moment think you had, but I wanted to be sure.'

'Well, now that you know I didn't, what are you going to do?'

'Severino is responsible for its loss, I

presume?' Lorenzo asked Claudia.

'I'm sure he won't deny taking it if we ask him,' she replied.

'Why did he do it?' Vanessa asked.

'I cannot always explain my father's actions. Perhaps he thought its loss would create a rift between Giovanni and myself, which in a roundabout way it did.'

'What do we do now?' Lorenzo asked.

'I will have words with my father, and I will make sure the ring is returned to Giovanni as soon as possible. I am sure I can concoct a story about it turning up somewhere or other. My ex-fiancé isn't exactly the brightest of men, so I don't suppose he will think my finding it amongst my belongings at all strange.'

'Where is he now, do you know?' Vanessa asked.

'In America.'

'And will you be staying on here?'

'Someone has to get some organisation about the place,' Claudia attempted a joke. 'Standards seem to have slipped since my last visit.'

'If you like, I'll do a quick check round outside to make sure everything's in order,' Lorenzo said, heading for the side door. 'Be back in a minute.'

Vanessa would have followed Lorenzo outside, but Claudia detained her. 'I presume the loss of the ring was why you moved in with my father and Jolly?'

'I needed to prove my innocence. I had to stay somewhere on the island. I was grateful when Severino offered me a room in the villa, but things got worse when the painting disappeared. I began to think I was jinxed.'

'Poor you,' Claudia sympathised. 'I will do my best to make things right for you, I promise. Why couldn't my father have been something normal like a bank manager?' She ran her hands through her hair with a gesture of mock despair. 'But I suppose if he was, I wouldn't love him half as much. Still, at least all this fuss has made me come to a decision. I am going to move back to Santa Agathe to keep a better eye on him.'

'What about your job?' Vanessa protested.

'I have resigned. That is why I was back early for Jolly's party. I have plans to market Severino as a brand. He will protest of course, but he will not stop me. Too many people have traded in on his name, and I am determined to put a stop to that. Marketing is what I am good at, so I intend to put my skills to good use.'

'Is your father your only reason for returning to the island?'

Beneath her tan, Claudia flushed. 'I don't know what you mean.'

'I think you'll find Jolly has her own plans in that direction.'

'You've lost me.' Claudia looked confused.

'Do you know she warned me off Carlo because Assunta told her he'd taken me out to lunch? Then she caught me peering through the window when he was hanging around outside. To cut a long story short — ' Vanessa waved away Claudia's attempt to interrupt. ' — I am doing a portrait of Assunta for Jolly's birthday. Of course I couldn't tell Jolly what was going on, as it's meant to be a surprise, but we had an awkward time of it until things got straightened out.'

Claudia continued to look uncomfortable.

'There's nothing between myself and Carlo other than a straightforward business arrangement.'

'Carlo and I grew up together,' Claudia said, waving away Vanessa's attempt to reassure her, 'but then our lives went in different directions. We kept in touch through Patricia, Carlo's wife, but there has never been anything of a romantic nature between us, even after Patricia's death. Right now I am not looking to fall into another relationship, but for the future — who knows?' she shrugged.

A loud thump outside, followed by a

muffled oath, caused both women to raise a reluctant smile. 'I think Lorenzo has had an unfortunate encounter with one of Papa's discarded canvases,' Claudia said.

Vanessa glanced at her watch. 'We should be leaving.'

Claudia put out a hand to detain her. 'Do you have plans for the future?'

'The ring has been found; the painting has been returned; you're moving back to the island; there's no reason for me to stay on in Santa Agathe.' It hurt Vanessa to admit the truth, but it had to be said.

'My father has taken a shine to you.' An impish smile curved the corners of Claudia's mouth. 'I can't always be around to handle him on my own.'

'You have Jolly, and I have my own work.'

'Painting portraits? You could do that anywhere, couldn't you?'

'I suppose I could. But why?'

'Severino can be difficult with people he doesn't like, even with me at times, and I am his daughter. I could do with some help.'

'I can't live off your father.'

'I'm not suggesting you do. It's a muddle at the moment, I know, but would you consider being my assistant in my new venture?'

'Doing what?'

'Helping me to sort out my crazy life? I know we didn't have the best of starts, but I really like you, and I'm sure given time we could become good friends. Please,' Claudia implored. 'I know I can trust you. Say you'll give it some thought.'

18

Children scampered after each other, squealing with delight in an energetic game of hide and seek. Jolly had been overjoyed with her present, and Assunta's portrait now occupied pride of place on one of Severino's easels. It was perilously close to the hide and seek path, and the group of admirers that was gathered around the portrait was doing its best to protect it whilst discussing its merits.

Jolly had been effusive in her thanks. 'Vanessa, you must develop your artwork,' she announced. 'Then the Maestro will have some serious competition.'

Claudia had interrupted the applause. 'One artist in the family is more than enough, Jolly. Besides, Vanessa is going to work for me as my new assistant.'

'That is splendid news.' Overhearing the exchange, Severino had been delighted. 'My two favourite girls together. What man could ask for more?' He embraced Vanessa warmly, showing surprising strength for a man of his years.

'Nothing has been decided yet,' insisted Vanessa, trying not very successfully to quell further applause.

'I have so many plans.' Claudia appeared to have inherited her father's trait of not listening to things that didn't interest her. 'We are going to be such a formidable team.'

'Claudia . . . ' But Vanessa's attempt to restrain her was also ignored.

'Papa, who are all these people?' Claudia demanded, turning her attention to the rising swell of guests. A steady crocodile was working its way down the drive from the security gates that had been left open in honour of the occasion. Jolly's party had been invitation only, but no one seemed to take any notice.

'They are my friends,' Severino insisted.

'You must know a lot of people.'

Raising her eyes to the sky, Claudia had allowed herself to be distracted by an art critic wanting to know about her plans to market the Severino brand.

'Why don't you take a break, Vanessa?' Jolly insisted. 'You have been on your feet all morning.'

'Only if you promise to rest up too. It's your birthday, remember?'

'I remember,' Jolly replied. 'And thank you for the beautiful silk scarf. I shall save it for special occasions.'

'Nonsense. Wear it now.' Severino whipped it off the back of the chair, where Jolly had placed it, and draped it around her neck. 'Doesn't she look beautiful?' he appealed to Carlo.

'My mother will always look beautiful,' he agreed. 'Now,' he said as he fussed around her, 'you heard Vanessa, Mama. Take the weight off your feet and let everyone else wait on you. Would you like some more cake?'

Still protesting, Jolly allowed Carlo to play the dutiful son.

Sensing a presence on the bench beside her, Vanessa instantly knew it was Lorenzo.

'Are you going to accept Claudia's offer?' he asked.

'I don't know,' she admitted, looking out across the harbour to where the Wild One overshadowed the proceedings, wisps of sulphuric smoke escaping the crater in gentle puffs.

'What is holding you back?'

'It would be a wrench to leave the island,' Vanessa admitted, uncertain how to answer Lorenzo's question.

'Is it your sister?'

'I owe Michelle a visit,' Vanessa replied, 'but she and Paulo need time to settle down to married life first.'

'Then what is troubling you?'

Vanessa wished she could ease Lorenzo's concern, but how could she explain? From the first day they had met, she had sensed Lorenzo would play a significant role in her life.

Michelle had also picked up on the chemistry between them. Vanessa had been so fired up over all that was going on, she hadn't bothered to take much notice of her sister, who saw romance round every corner; but there was no avoiding the truth. Lorenzo had put his job on the line for Vanessa — several times.

When she had blackmailed him into dancing the tango with her, he had risen to the challenge; he had rescued her from Giovanni's clutches when their host had suggested an intimate nightcap in the privacy of his cabin, then he had stood by her side when accusations of theft were being made against all those on board *The Riviera*.

Yet apart from that one kiss that had so excited Jolly's attention, there had been nothing between them. Vanessa knew her feelings for Lorenzo had grown and deepened. How could she know if he felt the same?

Aware that he was still looking expectantly at her, Vanessa plucked an excuse out of thin air. 'I can't help feeling Giovanni might still make trouble, and that could place Claudia in an awkward situation.'

'He's got his ring back, and Claudia kept your name out of it, didn't she?'

'Yes, but which name?'

'Does it matter?'

'It might do in the future.'

'People will soon forget, and you can't let one single incident ruin the rest of your life.'

'I suppose not.'

'And Claudia does deserve an answer.'

'Do you think I don't know that?' Vanessa's irritation rose to the surface. 'Sorry,' she backtracked. 'I just wish everyone wouldn't keep making up my mind for me.'

'It's because we care,' Lorenzo spoke in a soft voice.

'Do you?' Vanessa hardly dare ask the question.

'Isn't it obvious? Look around. Why do you think everyone was so pleased when Claudia said she had offered you a job?'

'I thought they were being polite.'

Lorenzo raised a disbelieving eyebrow. 'Santa Agathens are the best people in the world, but if they don't like you they don't do polite. Can't you see they've taken you to their hearts?'

'And I feel the same way about them. I've only been here a short time, but the island feels like home.'

'Then decision made. You must stay on.' Lorenzo frowned. 'Unless it's Claudia that's worrying you.'

'Claudia?'

'You like her, don't you?'

'Very much. Away from Giovanni, she's such a different person. She's kind, funny, and patient with her father. She's understanding and forgiving. I mean he did take the ring, so technically he's as guilty as the students who borrowed his painting.'

'Best not ruin your new relationship with Claudia by telling her that one,' Lorenzo advised.

'What will you do now?' Vanessa steeled herself to ask.

Lorenzo stretched out his long legs and crossed his arms. 'I have plans too. I'm going to set up a consultancy.'

'Here on the island?'

'Here on the island,' he acknowledged.

'Doing what?'

'Advising people on the best way to ensure their personal safety. Basics, really. Things like identity theft, online presence, password protection ... simple stuff like that can be easily overlooked but is equally as important as household security.' He paused. 'Did you know Claudia owns several properties on Santa Agathe?'

'No, I didn't.'

'She rents them out as holiday lets, and she's offered me the use of a villa on the coast road. It's a little out of the centre, but,' he added with a ghost of a smile, 'I have the use of a bicycle.'

Before Vanessa could reply, Severino bustled over. 'Claudia tells me you have not made up your mind to stay. You have to,' he insisted, waving a brush at her. 'If you do not, I shall never paint again — not another stroke — and you will be to blame. Claudia will be unable to market the Severino brand, and we shall all die poor and unloved. Can you live with that?'

'Papa,' Claudia chided, 'don't be so dramatic, and don't make idle threats.'

'I mean every word,' he insisted. 'To think, Vanessa, I gave you my heart, and this is the way you repay me.'

Heads began to turn in their direction, making Vanessa feel extremely uncomfortable. 'Please, Severino,' she implored.

He turned his back on her. 'I am not talking to you. Never again will I speak to you.'

Claudia pulled a sympathetic face. 'My father must really like you, Vanessa. He only argues like this with people he loves.'

Her words caused a lump to lodge in Vanessa's throat. 'Can't you talk him round?' she implored Claudia.

'Papa,' Claudia said, taking hold of his hand, 'you know you do not wish to paint a sequel to *Il Pomeriggio*.'

'I never said any such thing.'

'Yes you did, so don't upset Vanessa by pretending otherwise.'

'She has upset me, wounded me deeply.'

'No she hasn't. It is a big step for her. Of course she has to think about it.'

'Thank you,' Vanessa mouthed at Claudia behind Severino's back.

'What can I do if I don't paint?' he said.

'You can run your workshops again, and give talks to students, and I will arrange guest appearances for you in the media.'

'I do not want to do that.'

'It's what marketing is all about. There will be lots of social occasions and new people to meet. You'd like that, wouldn't you?'

'Only if Vanessa is with me,' he insisted with a stubborn look on his face. 'She understands art. That is why I love her.'

'Vanessa?' Claudia looked as though she was doing her best not to sound desperate.

'I have another good idea,' Severino announced, his good humour bouncing back. 'Vanessa can stay in your villa with Lorenzo.'

'No, Severino,' Vanessa said, deciding it was time to be firm with him. 'I couldn't.'

'I'm up for it,' Lorenzo put in.

'Stop putting ideas in everyone's head.' Vanessa glared at him.

'If you're going to be tediously conventional,' Severino sighed, 'then I suppose you had better get married first. But don't leave it too long, and hurry up, and have some babies too. Lorenzo, propose to Vanessa immediately.'

'Papa, stop being troublesome,' Claudia chided.

'I am never troublesome,' he insisted. 'And as for you, young lady, you had better hurry up and marry your Carlo. We could make it a double ceremony.'

By now both Vanessa and Claudia were as red-faced as each other.

'I have no intention of marrying Carlo or anyone else, and you're to stop teasing Vanessa.'

'Jolly?' Severino appealed to his housekeeper. 'You agree with me, don't you? We could have a double ceremony.'

'What is all this talk of marriage?' Having enjoyed a brief rest, Jolly was now up on her feet, juggling large plates of cake in her capable hands.

There was no stopping Severino now. 'Vanessa and Lorenzo, and Claudia and Carlo, have announcements to make.'

'No we do not,' both women protested at the same time.

'They are getting married? That is wonderful news. Claudia, why didn't you tell me?'

In her excitement, Jolly dropped her plates of cake. Crushing the contents underfoot, she embraced Claudia. 'My darling child, you will make a perfect daughter-in-law. It has always been my dearest wish that one day you and my Carlo would marry.'

'Lorenzo,' Vanessa hissed, 'do something. Things are getting out of control.'

'You want me to propose to you now, in front of everybody?'

Vanessa almost lost her footing as she stepped back. 'That's not what I meant, and you know it. There's no talking to you. No one's listening to anything I have to say.' Turning, Vanessa blundered into numerous guests as she pushed her way through a sea of curious faces.

'Where are you going?' Lorenzo called after her.

Vanessa hurried down the winding path, praying Lorenzo would not come after her. The doors were wide open and she plunged into the darkened studio, welcoming the coolness of the atmosphere. She placed a canvas chair in front of *Il Pomeriggio* and sank into it.

Severino was impossible. Not only had he placed her in an intolerable situation, but he had made it impossible for her to accept Claudia's offer. She could never face Lorenzo again.

The beauty of Severino's masterpiece began to calm her racing nerves. *The Harbour at Sunset* was placed beside *Il Pomeriggio*, and Vanessa could feel the familiar lump of emotion rising in her chest as she looked at the two examples of the artist's great work. Her life without him would be much less colourful.

A shadow blotted out the sun behind her and a voice enquired, 'Do you mind if I join you?'

'Carlo.' Vanessa smiled in relief, fearing the visitor might have been Lorenzo, or worse, Severino. Carlo sat down beside Vanessa. 'Have you come to escape from the family too?' she asked.

'My mother won't hear a word against Severino,' Carlo admitted with a wry twist to his lips, 'but at times he can be impossible. I think he uses his artistic temperament to get away with being outrageous. But then I suppose we wouldn't have him any other way either.'

'What are you going to do about Claudia?' Vanessa asked.

'I have absolutely no idea. I left Claudia and Severino engaged in a heated dispute. I've been through this situation so many times, my advice is take a back seat until things have calmed down.'

'Do they — calm down?'

'Eventually.'

'You and Claudia?' Vanessa ventured. 'I don't mean to pry,' she hastened to add.

'I didn't realise I was in love with Claudia until she got engaged to Giovanni. Then it was too late.'

'And now?'

'I don't know.'

'I know Claudia's saying she has no intention of getting engaged again, but Giovanni wasn't right for her. You are.' Vanessa smiled self-consciously. 'I'm beginning to sound like everybody else around here, aren't I? Interfering, offering advice where it's not wanted?'

'I could give you the same advice about Lorenzo. He's a good man. Go for it.'

They lapsed into companionable silence while the sun beat down on the terrace outside.

'You know,' Carlo said as he moved his chair forward to closer inspect *Il Pomeriggio*, 'I think I've got it.'

'Sorry?' Lost in thought, Vanessa jumped at the sound of his excited voice.

'There.' He pointed to Severino's signature on *Il Pomeriggio*. 'It was staring us in the face all the time.'

'What was?'

'When the sun moved angle, I saw it.'

'Saw what?'

'Can't you see it?'

'No.'

'It's different.'

'What is?'

'The signature. It looks black, but when the light changes it's dark blue.

You've got to look hard, but I'm not mistaken, am I? It's all to do with the angle of the sun in the studio.'

'Carlo, you've cracked it.'

Vanessa leapt to her feet and threw her arms around his neck. Over his shoulder, her eyes crashed into those of Lorenzo.

19

She pushed Carlo away.

'What's the matter?' he asked, seeing the look of dismay on her face.

'Carlo?' Claudia now stood beside Lorenzo. Before he could reply, she turned swiftly on her heel.

'I'd better go after her.' Carlo made a gesture of apology with his shoulders. 'I'll break our news to Severino, shall I?'

Lorenzo looked as shocked as Claudia. 'How long has this been going on?' he demanded.

'Nothing's going on,' Vanessa replied.

'Jolly was right all along, wasn't she?'

'No.'

'You owe it to Claudia as well to tell her the true reason for your reluctance to accept her offer, although how you are going to break the news to Jolly I shudder to think. And as for

Severino . . . ' his voice trailed off.

'If you could only hear yourself,' Vanessa said, her self-control breaking down. 'So what if I was embracing Carlo? What is it to you?'

A dull red flush worked its way up Lorenzo's neck. 'It's nothing to me. I was thinking of Claudia.'

'Why? She and Carlo aren't officially an item, are they, despite Severino's mischief-making? Or have I missed something?'

'Only this.' Lorenzo took a step forward and, sweeping Vanessa into his arms, kissed her. If his hand had not been supporting the small of her back, she strongly suspected she would have collapsed onto Severino's masterpiece.

'What do you think you're doing?' she demanded, recovering enough to push him away.

'Something I've held off from doing far too long.'

'Why?'

'Look out.' Lorenzo gave her shoulders an angry wrench as she now came within a hair's breadth of knocking *The Harbour at Sunset* off its easel. 'You're in enough trouble without wrecking a Severino work of art.'

'So are you.' Vanessa's throat hurt to speak. 'In deep trouble.'

'What have I done?'

'Jumped to the most illogical, stupid conclusions about Carlo and me.'

'You can't deny you were in Carlo's arms.'

'No, I can't, and I expect poor old Carlo is having a similar conversation with Claudia right now. If you hold your breath, I'll tell you exactly what was going on, and then you can tell me why you kissed me.'

In the distance, Vanessa could hear music. Someone started to sing amid cheers and the chinking of glasses.

'It sounds as though the party has settled down,' Vanessa added in a softer voice. 'So once we're through here, we could go and join in the celebrations.'

Indecision swept across Lorenzo's face. 'You and Carlo?' he ground out through gritted teeth.

'We both had the same idea and came down here to get away from Jolly and Severino.'

'Because Severino suggested we should get married, an idea that was so unwelcome you ran away from it. And now I know the reason why.'

'I came down here because — ' Vanessa looked helplessly at the paintings lining the walls. ' — I couldn't bear it any longer.'

'Bear what?'

'The thought of leaving Santa Agathe and you.'

'You expect me to believe that?'

'It's the truth.'

'You've a fine way of showing it.'

'Carlo and I were embracing because we discovered that Severino signed his work in a different shade of paint on *Il Pomeriggio*. And if you don't believe me, take a look.'

Lorenzo's eyes flickered towards one of the canvases. 'I can't see it.'

'That's because you have to wait for

the light to change. It probably only happens once a day. That's why no one noticed it before. Incredible to believe, but they probably weren't looking at it at the right time or in the right place.' Vanessa crossed her arms. 'Now it's your turn.'

'To do what?'

'To tell me why you kissed me.'

Lorenzo took a step towards her. 'I followed you down here to try to persuade you to stay.'

'Why?'

Lorenzo ran a hand through his hair. 'Why do you think I've been inventing excuses to keep you on the island?'

'By calling me a thief?'

'If you want to put it like that, yes. I had no power to detain you. I knew you were innocent. It doesn't take a genius to work out that if you were guilty, you would have been on the first flight out. I knew your sister was far too scatty to be involved in a robbery; and when she stood up for you from the off, I figured the pair of you had to be innocent.'

Out of the corner of her eye, Vanessa could see groups beginning to dance as someone upped the tempo of the music. 'Where does all this leave us?' she asked.

'I hope you are going to follow Carlo's example, Lorenzo,' Severino, standing in the doorway, said in a tired voice. 'And hurry up about it, because I need some rest. Carlo has proposed to Claudia,' he explained. 'And despite displaying initial reluctance, she has accepted him. But I have told her no more ghastly engagement rings. She is to have a plain solitaire diamond. Jolly and I agree that is far more suitable.'

'I see you've thought of everything,' Vanessa murmured.

'Not quite,' Severino replied. He turned to Lorenzo. 'You are in love with Vanessa?'

'I've been trying to convince her I am, but it's not easy.'

'She's spirited, my Vanessa.' Severino smiled. 'But she is in love with you. I'm an artist; I can see it in her eyes. So,

Vanessa, I hope you are going to make me a happy man by agreeing you are also in love with Lorenzo?'

Vanessa looked from Severino, to Lorenzo, then back to Severino. 'I am,' she admitted.

Severino took the news calmly. 'In that case, if you don't mind, I would like my studio back. Go and join the others, and tell Carlo I may never speak to him again now he has uncovered my little secret.'

'Are we engaged?' Lorenzo murmured in Vanessa's ear as Severino closed his studio doors firmly behind them, leaving them standing on the terrace.

'According to Severino we are, but you haven't actually proposed to me,' Vanessa pointed out.

'Will you marry me? As soon as possible?' Lorenzo sounded urgent.

'Whenever you like.' Vanessa smiled into his eyes.

In the distance, the Wild One gave a contented puff of smoke.

FESTIVAL FEVER
LOVE WILL FIND A WAY
HUNGRY FOR LOVE

We do hope that you have enjoyed reading this large print book.

Did you know that all of our titles are available for purchase?

We publish a wide range of high quality large print books including:
Romances, Mysteries, Classics
General Fiction
Non Fiction and Westerns

Special interest titles available in large print are:
The Little Oxford Dictionary
Music Book, Song Book
Hymn Book, Service Book

Also available from us courtesy of Oxford University Press:
Young Readers' Dictionary
(large print edition)
Young Readers' Thesaurus
(large print edition)

For further information or a free brochure, please contact us at:
Ulverscroft Large Print Books Ltd.,
The Green, Bradgate Road, Anstey,
Leicester, LE7 7FU, England.
Tel: (00 44) **0116 236 4325**
Fax: (00 44) **0116 234 0205**

GRAND DESIGNS

Linda Mitchelmore

Interior decorator Carrie Fraser cannot believe her luck when she is invited to work at beautiful Oakenbury Hall. Nor can she quite get over the owner of the Hall, the gorgeous and wealthy Morgan Harrington. Morgan is bound by his late father's wishes to keep Oakenbury within the family and have children; and the more time Carrie spends with him, the more she yearns to be the woman to fulfil this wish. But the likes of Carrie Fraser could never be enough for a high-flying businessman like Morgan . . . could she?

A WESTERN HEART

Liz Harris

Wyoming, 1880: Childhood sweethearts Rose McKinley and Will Hyde have always been destined to marry; and with their parents just as keen on the match, there is nothing to stop them. Except perhaps Cora, Rose's younger sister. Lovesick and hung up on Will, she is fed up with the happy couple. So when the handsome Mr Galloway comes to town and turns Rose's head, Cora sees an opportunity to get what she wants: Will . . .

ISLAND MAGIC

Vanessa Blake's sister asks her to take her place as dance professional on a private yacht owned by the Petucci family — then promptly disappears. When a priceless ring goes missing on the yacht, Vanessa realises she is high on the list of suspects. Taking refuge on the island of Santa Agathe, she thinks she is safe — until a valuable painting by local artist Severino, with whom she is staying, is stolen. Can Vanessa trust security chief Lorenzo Talbot to help prove her innocence, or does he have his own agenda?